THE CAPTAIN'S TABLE

Brian Thompson

WINDSOR
PARAGON

First published 2009
by Chatto & Windus
This Large Print edition published 2009
by BBC Audiobooks Ltd
by arrangement with
Atlantic Books

Hardcover ISBN: 978 1 408 41439 2
Softcover   ISBN: 978 1 408 41440 8

British Library Cataloguing in Publication Data available

Printed and bound in Great Britain by
CPI Antony Rowe, Chippenham and Eastbourne

CHAPTER ONE

London, one late August afternoon in 1876. Hyde Park is busy with people, the better sort strolling on the dusty paths, herding their children gently in front of them. From time to time these family groups are overtaken by men in frock coats who have given up their carriages and are taking the air at a brisk pace. In this way one might encounter someone like Lord Hartington of the War Office, moving at a suitably military clip and trailing two or three secretaries behind him. At the sound of the great man's approach—and Hartington does not stint but comes on like a cheery yet urgent tornado—gentlemen raise their hats, the parasols part and boys in sailor suits stand to attention. The better sort (or maybe only the more impudent) salute.

So it is also along the sanded carriage drive that runs around the edge of the park. On a mild and windless day such as this is, men of affairs, peers of the realm, half-pay admirals, dowager duchesses and distinguished foreigners roll gently past under the trees. The public likes to congregate in knots to watch them. There is a sudden flurry of hat-raising—the Queen's youngest son, Prince Leopold, is seen to be taking the air, looking well, according to some bystanders, looking drawn and hunted to others. The ladies with him in the royal landau are identified as Lady Breadalbane and Sir Henry Ponsonby's good-natured wife, Mary.

Prince Leopold's mama, if she ever got wind of such innocent pleasures, would at once put a stop

1

to them: she has it in her head that her boy is an incurable invalid, quite as likely to fall out of his carriage as to enjoy its easy motion. As everyone knows, there is something wrong with his blood and even the slightest accident with scissors might threaten his life. He has the anguished sympathy of those who watch. There is a scattering of applause and one or two muted huzzas. A recent story tells how, when in Oxford for the funeral of Dean Liddell's dearest daughter, Leopold took a white rose from his buttonhole and laid it on the coffin. There was gallantry in this gesture but also some real emotion. None of Victoria's other sons could have done such a thing—or not with such unassuming grace.

The Prince, who has impeccable manners, raises his hat a little, just a very little, at the warm reception given to his carriage. His smile is soft and diffident. Lady Ponsonby, who sees everything and knows everyone, dips her head in grateful acknowledgement of the crowd's kindness. Tonight, a hundred or so gentle souls will speak about their encounter with Prince Leopold as though he had stepped from the carriage and shaken each of them by the hand. This pale haemophiliac, with a student's beard and uncertain blue eyes, is somehow their connection to what makes England great.

*   *   *

But by far the larger number in the park today are men and women from another world altogether. They sprawl, they drink, they fornicate. Hundreds of empty bottles reflect the sun and the dusty grass is stiff with broken glass. From time to time the police sprint after thieves or form in knots to prevent a breach of public order, as, for example, when a ragged file of former soldiers pass, playing battered instruments. They are almost too drunk to stand, these men, and their behaviour insults the few scraps of uniform they wear. Their intention is to reach the mamas and their children, the better to wring their hearts. The police have drawn truncheons to prevent them.

There are people here who have been turned off from distant factories, agricultural labourers who have not seen work for months, dismissed servants, French and German exiles, beggars, whores and bully boys. The hubbub that is carried on the sultry breeze comes in part from hundreds of them bathing in the Serpentine, as near naked as makes no difference, roaring like seals, copulating, occasionally fighting, just like seals.

Foreign visitors are amazed by these sights, but to Londoners it is just another day in the park. In Berlin, in the Tiergarten, such a spectacle as these nameless and faceless beasts that roam and bicker on the tawny grass would be unimaginable. In Paris, the Jardin du Luxembourg is cleansed of the unwelcome and the unwaged by that same French sense of propriety that also ensures the pollarded trees are as near identical as possible and the iron benches aligned like parade soldiers.

Here in London, the rich pass among the poor with something like equanimity. Mortice locks and insurance policies are one form of defence; that nebulous idea, the Law (meaning the courts of justice, the treadmill, bread and water) another. Most of all, a Londoner of the better class will tell

3

you that it is only very occasionally one has to meet the lower classes face to face. Even a hundred yards makes a difference.

The afternoon wears on, the parasols twink and slowly disappear. In an hour or two the roads around the park will be filled with traffic on its way to very different addresses. In some of the more popular streets and squares, there will be a queue of vehicles waiting to discharge elegant and perfumed guests, not at a little distance from their destinations, but immediately outside the front door. The human animals with whom they shared the afternoon are forgotten. This is a different— and most would say—a better world.

*　　　*　　　*

On this particular autumn day, Mrs Bella Wallis was saying goodbye to her godson, Jack. Earlier they had been to Shepherd's studio in Long Acre, where the boy was photographed in his spanking new ensign's uniform, doing his best to look worldly and as far as was possible, languid, one arm cocked against a white glaze jardinière. His right boot was planted on the head that decorated a tiger rug and an occasional table bore books and a rolled map. Young though he looked, he carried off this make-believe well, with one sorry exception. The moustache he had been ordered to grow by his adjutant was too sparse and pale for the camera: with the greatest tact Mr Shepherd suggested some judicious darkening. There were blushes and indignation at this but Bella held his chin firm and applied a very little rouge, so that Ensign Starling was captured for posterity in his

4

blues, a thirty-guinea sword at just the right angle, his boot on a tiger's head—and a red streak across his upper lip.

'You look very well, sir,' Shepherd smiled. 'If I may say so, a credit to your regiment.'

'He sails for Capetown tonight,' Bella said, busying herself with a handkerchief at Jack's upper lip. Though she had been a widow for more than ten years, and had not seen her godson for five, she could all the same feel the heat of childish lust coming off him. His excited breath fanned her cheeks. Bella sighed. The new subaltern, like most of his kind, was a danger to shipping.

She offered him early dinner at Fracatelli's but he asked instead to go back with her to the house in Orange Street. As they walked, he gave her his arm.

'You really are most incredibly beautiful,' the boy blurted as they crossed the road into St Martin's Lane. Bella laughed.

'Why, Jack, that isn't often said of me.'

'I should so like to kiss you.'

'May we not take the thought for the deed?'

He followed her glance and saw a dishevelled figure saluting them both. The man wore a faded red tunic of ancient cut and concertina canvas trousers. Dundreary whiskers decorated a face heated by drink. To amuse passers-by (at any rate to his own satisfaction) he was marching with one foot in the gutter and one on the pavement.

'Who is that?' Jack asked, alarmed.

'I have no idea,' his godmother said in a very guarded tone.

'But he seems to know you. If not, if he is merely being importunate, allow me to deal with him.'

5

'You'll do no such thing.'

The old soldier, if that is what he was, laid his finger along his nose, straightened his back and executed an extravagant right-wheel into New Row. Jack stared after him in amazement.

'That fellow has the impudence of the devil.'

'Yes,' Bella agreed grimly.

'But does he know you?'

'His name is Quigley, these are his streets and he has quite as much right to walk in them as anyone else. And you, my dear, are nineteen years old, take ship for Africa later on tonight and must try to learn not to be such a confounded owl.'

'I beg your pardon,' Jack said, perking up his chin and blushing to the roots of his hair.

Though he knew London hardly at all, Orange Street was not very much his idea of a good address. Starling had been warned by his mother that dear, dear Bella was quite the woman of mystery, which to Mrs Starling was the same as saying she had a wooden leg. The faintly raucous street Bella lived in was mystery enough to Jack, as was the house itself, shabby on the outside but wonderfully calm and elegant within. Bella's drawing room was small but—to his young eyes—perfect. The blue-grey walls were set off by some very good paintings. Once seated (or sprawled, remembering to cross his legs at the ankle as did all the fellows in the mess) he was calmed by a glass of very good claret and the present she made him of a leather writing wallet.

'I wish to apologise for my earlier behaviour,' he said with stiff formality.

Bella jumped up and kissed him on his forehead. 'You are such a chump, dearest Jack. We are friends, as much as more or less complete strangers can be. By midnight tonight you will quite forget me. That is entirely as it should be. In three weeks' time you will be at the Cape, cutting a dash with your fellow officers and letting the adjutant win at billiards.'

He laughed. What he saw in front of him was a woman in her early forties, with wonderfully grey eyes and a humorous mouth. There was a magic about her, not least because she lived alone with the sort of self-possession his own mother lacked completely. The dusty old fool they had stumbled across in St Martin's Lane was a poser, to be sure: what on earth was his godmother doing by being able to name such a dreg? But there was a bud of commonsense in Ensign Jack Starling that would grow and blossom in time—far, far beyond this present moment—to adorn a general's rank. He saw that he was dealing with a real person and not some cypher.

He toasted her across the rim of his glass. 'Well,' he said gallantly, 'I apologise for wanting to kiss you but insist upon describing you as the most beautiful woman I have ever met.'

'Spoken like a gentleman.'

And then he was gone, in a flurry of cabs and trunks. It would not have broken his heart but might have piqued him to know that within an hour the beautiful Bella Wallis had more or less forgotten his existence. She read, she yawned, she ate a plate of cold cuts; and as the night drew in, lit lamps. In order not to shock her godson she had abstained from smoking in his presence but now she lay back in her favourite chair with her shoes kicked off and a cheroot smouldering in a saucer.

7

The boy Jack was her sister-in-law's child, from happier days. Then Bella had lived in some style in Hertfordshire with her husband Garnett. When he died, she moved back to London and set about reinventing herself, not as a society lady and certainly not as a grieving widow. There were no children of the marriage and not much money left to her in Garnett's will. She lived quietly. Though for a giddy year or so she was embroiled—and that was the very word for it—with the beautiful and childlike Marie Claude D'Anville, represented to the wider world as her companion, Bella Wallis was one of those lucky people who have an exact idea of who they are.

She was someone who could live alone and not shrivel like an apple. Marie Claude was gone, more or less amicably; and while there were plenty of men only too willing to take her place, Bella enjoyed her own company. There was a pleasure to be got from listening, as now, to the sighing of the house as it settled for the night: the bumps and creaks and faint gurgle of water in the pipes that was as familiar to her as conversation.

'Ah, but where are her wellsprings?' an intelligent woman had once asked. 'What is the source of this perpetual refreshment?'

No one knew. At eleven by the clock, Bella flung her arms back over her head to ease her spine and walked upstairs, unbuttoning as she went. She unpinned her hair, scooped water into her face and eyes, completed her undressing and slipped naked into bed.

If there was one being who could bring down the walls she had built around herself, whose genial good nature could beguile her more than any other

8

man she had ever known (and that included her late husband), he was not in London tonight, and probably not in England either. Philip Westland shared her own knack of seeming to walk alone. They were lovers in the strictly technical sense—an exuberantly romantic weekend in Shropshire—but had circled each other since like sun and moon.

Bella fell asleep with his name upon her lips. And then woke at two, cursed roundly, padded downstairs and found—by feeling gently along the mantelpiece—a pasteboard invitation. She took it upstairs in the dark and laid it on the second pillow to remind herself in the morning, before diving once more into dreamless sleep.

As for Jack Starling, he lay on his back in a cabin hardly bigger than a wardrobe, his mouth filled with bile and about as far from sleep as was the English Channel from the Cape of Good Hope. A choppy head sea, though it barely troubled the massive three-decker he was sailing in, had uncorked smells that did nothing for the stomach. For three hours he had taken his farewell of dear old England with his head in a tin basin.

*   *   *

Bella was both right and wrong about Philip Westland's whereabouts. He was out of England but on his way home. He was in fact in Calais, talking none too willingly with a man called Alcock from the British Embassy in Paris. Alcock was a former naval commander with some of the brusquerie of that profession.

'You saw our friend in Cognac, I believe,' he suggested.

9

'I saw the man you sent me to meet, yes.'

Westland's attraction to both men and women was a shambolic sort of charm. He was tall but maybe a stone or so overweight. His expression was frank and unflinching but could be misunderstood as slow-wittedness. Alcock, for example, who suffered under the delusion that he could tell a man's worth by the way he picked up a wineglass, or a spoon, considered Westland a bit of an ox.

'How was he?' he persisted. 'How was our friend?'

'I wonder why you keep calling him our friend,' Westland mused. 'The feeling is not reciprocated. But, to answer your question, he is very well aware of the interest taken in him and responded accordingly.'

'Ha! He was on the qui vive, shall we say?'

'I think weary resignation is a better description.'

'There is a young wife, I believe?'

'There is indeed. Her name is Laetitia.'

Alcock chewed his lip for a moment or two.

'You gave him the Ambassador's letter?'

'I gave him the letter you gave me. I might as well have given him a handful of gravel scooped from the hotel grounds. I must tell you, Commander Alcock, I am about as fitted for this sort of business as a one-legged bosun.'

'Bosun? Why do you say bosun?' Alcock cried sharply.

'Don't the best bosuns have two legs?'

Alcock lit a cigarette. This fellow Westland was either some sort of simpleton or had just said something very deep. 'You have managed a very small but quite significant piece of intrigue for your country,' he explained. 'And I think you should be proud. I will not trouble you further tonight, Mr Westland. I believe you catch the early boat?'

'That is so.'

'I hope we may call on your services again.'

'Oh, I shouldn't bother,' Philip Westland murmured. 'The French postal services can do as well, or better. And, of course, with them you get to keep the stamp.'

The man's an idiot, Commander Alcock decided. This impression was reinforced when they stood to shake hands. Westland overtopped him by more than a foot. He would not do, the commander noted to himself. Would not do at all.

CHAPTER TWO

'I go to Lady Cornford's tonight, Mrs Venn,' Bella said, tracking her housekeeper to the cellars, where that good woman had strung washing lines, as if sheets needed dark to dry them. She was mangling by the light that came through a dusty grille and singing hymns to keep her spirits up. There was a very pleasant smell of damp linen and palm oil soap, as well as coal dust and lime.

'I have a piece of stewing steak that needs cooking,' Mrs Venn warned. 'Shall you have that when you come home? In a small pie, with mushrooms?'

'Well, I think not. Tomorrow, perhaps.'

'You don't eat enough to gratify a bee.'

11

'So I have heard you say, often. But the mushrooms sound appealing.'

'From some old country boy selling door to door. Speaking in such a Hertfordshire accent, you could cut it with a knife. Though I don't say as how the shrooms come from those parts.'

'Not too likely,' Bella agreed, edging towards the cellar steps.

'But a decent enough old country character. Leather gaiters and all, you know. And only trying to earn a crust, like the rest of us.'

Bella paused with one foot on the stone stairs. 'Was there something else you wanted to say, Mrs Venn?'

'It is not my part to say anything,' the housekeeper confessed shyly. 'I know that—and may the Lord guide my words now. I will say what is in my heart. I cannot bear to see you lonely, Mrs Wallis.'

Bella walked back into the gloom and embraced her right there by the mangle and—for good measure—kissed her on her burning cheek. Then, being sensible women both of them, they burst out laughing.

What to wear, however? Cissie Cornford liked her men to appear in white tie, which more or less forced the ladies into full evening gowns. Since many of her female acquaintance were elderly, like herself, it was almost an imposition upon younger guests to show rather more bosom than they might wish. Snowy bosoms and bare arms, a little jewellery from the family inheritance—these made anyone under fifty a ready topic of conversation. Beady-eyed old dames studied the figures, dress and deportment of certain guests—particularly the unwary, or the impudent—with mumbling relish. Wrong necklace, I think! My dear, quite the wrong colour gloves! And so on.

Bella left the house in one of her favourite outfits, a pale blue dress with a short train and the least concession possible to the line created by the obligatory bustle. Her jewellery was antique, to be sure, but did not come down from her mother. The necklace of exquisitely cut turquoise had first been seen at the opening night of Rossini's *William Tell* in another country altogether and recovered fifty years later from a boutique in Paris by the most adorable man in Britain. More's the pity he was not there to admire it, nor to fix the tricky clasp.

*   *   *

Lady Cecily Cornford's house was located in Bedford Square. To the virtues of a tall and chaste Georgian design were added gates that protected the square itself; and in the centre a locked garden, seldom entered. Many a tradesman cursed when having to deliver goods to Bedford Square, because under the terms of the leasehold, drays and vans were not admitted. Everything, from a bouquet of flowers to a ton of coals had to be carried in by hand. Sofas, like pianos, followed the same pavement route.

Cissie Cornford, if she thought about it at all, considered these arrangements perfectly normal. To her mind, all London was shaped by iron railings and marble doorsteps. How else would people choose to live? She seldom ventured beyond Bloomsbury, and since the death of her husband cultivated an eccentricity she was sure was

13

nobody's business but her own. It had one pleasing consequence, however. Every month she gave a chaotic at-home that her more loyal friends talked of as Cissie Cornford's salon. This was a description she disliked.

'It's buns and bounce,' she explained with a vague wave of her hand. 'And of course, the servants adore it.'

If they did, they moved from guest to guest without too much bounce of their own. The youngest was sixty. Their task, as explained by the butler, was to stop her ladyship from setting fire to the place, for a feature of these evenings was the colossal number of lamps and candelabra scattered about the principal rooms. Already that night, Lady Yeadon had cause to be extinguished by a soda syphon, when exhibiting the pronation required to bow a cello properly. The lace cuff to her sleeve had burst into tiny flames.

'How terribly, terribly tiresome. Tell me, my dear,' Cissie continued blithely, quizzing her friend Bella Wallis with a solicitude that was far too tender to be genuine, 'do you ever hear anything of that frightful scrub Westland?'

Bella accepted a sugared almond from the plate proffered her by Lady Cornford's pride and joy, her Scottish servant Rankin, and held it expertly between her thumb and forefinger. She managed to stay calm by superhuman effort.

'Is he such a scrub?' she asked.

'My poor child, they say he is in Baden Baden at this very moment, along with a French comtesse old enough to be his mother.'

'I had heard Mr Westland was in Rome.'

'Do you say so? He is a spy, is he not?'

14

'A spy!' Bella exclaimed. 'A moment ago you were telling me he was a philandering scrub.'

'Someone whispered something along those lines to me recently, I am sure. Who was it? I declare my mind is like a sieve these days. Ah, there is Sir William Skillane just come in with his wife and daughter. Do talk to them: nobody else will, I am sure.'

For the moment, Bella was left stranded in almost the centre of the carpet, contemplating the idea of Philip Westland moving like a shadow through the streets of Vienna, or wherever spies congregated. It was an absurd image but one with just enough itchy persistence to prevent her laughing aloud. Indeed, she frowned. She had hardly expected the name to come up at all and inside her bodice her heart was pounding.

Cissie Cornford's drawing room held forty people comfortably. The guest of honour for this particular soirée was the painter William Frith, recently returned from Italy. Though he was not yet sixty, Frith, an inveterate clubman, liked to play up the image of the genial old buffer. Many of his anecdotes had correspondingly hoary whiskers. People found him amusing because he took so much naive pleasure in the jokes he told.

Cissie had been right about the Skillanes. They stood just inside the drawing room's double doors, as awkward as railway passengers waiting for the down train. Frith was on song and they arrived just at the moment that a gale of laughter swept the room. Sir William Skillane regarded the painter with unsmiling suspicion.

'Has he anything about him?' he asked Bella. 'I have heard of him, but is he any good? That's the

15

first question I ask of any man.'

He said this in such a loud voice and with such repellent unction that others nearby turned their heads and Bella herself flinched. Skillane wore evening dress with an easy air and sported a grey silk ribbon around his neck, at the end of which dangled some kind of foreign decoration. Most of the people in the room considered this a mark of the utmost vulgarity: Sir William liked to draw attention to his geegaw by constant touching. His hair and beard were snowy white and his eyes a watery blue. To look at someone, he had the habit of lifting his chin and sighting along a huge beak nose no wider than a knife blade.

'Now, there is a fellow I would not take to sea, no, not for a million in cash.'

'Mr Frith will be sorely disappointed to hear it,' Bella said. 'And you, Lady Skillane, would you sit to the artist?'

Agnes Skillane shook her head, wringing her hands. 'I don't believe we know too many people here,' she whispered, peering about her in agony.

'You are from Cornwall, I think.'

'And Cadogan Square,' her husband added with a smirk.

'Yes, indeed.'

It seemed the only sane Skillane was the daughter, Mary, who looked at Bella with such an air of pleading that the older woman took pity on her and led her off to meet Mr Eddinshaw, who was writing the parish history of Marylebone. Eddinshaw was earnest, youthful, and almost completely otherworldly. The two were made for each other. They fled to the furthermost corner of the room, behind the piano.

16

'Who is that uncouth giant with the white beard?' Billy Frith asked Bella a few minutes later. 'Is he an actor of some kind?'

'His name is Sir William Skillane. From Cornwall and Cadogan Square.'

'Good God,' Frith said reverently. 'What is that you are holding in your hand?'

'A sugared almond.'

The painter took it from her and dropped it into a floral decoration. 'They say that Bancroft might pitch up later. I very much hope so. I make of you an honourable exception but the rest of the crowd here are as alluring as scabbed sheep. I can't persuade you to jump on the table and dance a wild fandango?'

'You cannot.'

'It would make a pretty sight. The most handsome woman I ever knew was the Duchess of Manchester, as she was in her youth. One morning—'

'Forgive me,' Bella pleaded, 'but this is a story you have told me many times.'

'You are right,' Frith said, after a glum pause. 'I forget what a very intelligent woman you are. And what a ghastly old windbag I have become.'

'Do you not see merit in Sir William's face, I mean in compositional terms?'

'I do not. He looks like a parakeet that has swallowed poisoned thistles. Is that the daughter who blushes so prettily?'

Bella glanced. A deep flush was rising from Mary Skillane's bosom and burning on her cheeks. Eddinshaw seemed oblivious to the effect he was having. Bella smiled at Billy Frith and made her way over.

17

'We shall have an ice together, Miss Skillane,' she proposed. 'Mr Eddinshaw can cool his heels here for a moment.'

'We have been talking about bills of mortality,' he explained.

'I can't think of a more engaging topic,' Bella assured him. When she laid her hand on Mary's forearm, she was amazed to find the girl was trembling.

'He asked me how things stood along those lines in Cornwall,' she whispered. 'I answered that I was sure we had nothing of such an advanced nature.'

'Whereabouts do you live in Cornwall?' Bella asked.

'St Ives. Well, not St Ives itself, of course, which is nothing but pilchards and chapels—' Miss Skillane's voice trailed off and she smiled wanly. 'I am quoting my father now. I have no gift for conversation, Mrs Wallis. Pilchards and chapels and . . . there was something else, but I have forgot.'

Another fiery blush. Bella began to fear the girl would faint clean away from nerves. She cast about for something to say that would not prostrate her.

'Which do you prefer, tell me? Cornwall or Cadogan Square?'

'I would be happy to be away from either,' Miss Skillane answered with very unexpected vehemence. 'Indeed, away from everything altogether.'

'Well, that is straight enough. I have had those same feelings from time to time.'

'You have?'

'From time to time. Listen, I will give you my card, Miss Skillane, and you shall call on me

18

whenever you are in need of idle conversation about hats, or shoes.'

'You are very kind,' the girl said. 'I know I should do better but I feel completely outfaced. So many intelligent people.'

'Most of whom would be delighted to meet you. Don't you go out in society at all?'

'Hardly at all,' Mary Skillane said.

'Do you read? Tell me what you are reading.'

'I know I should mention something improving but we are not much of a reading family. My mother has just finished a novel called *The Widow's Secret*.'

'Ah yes,' Bella said with guarded amusement. 'And how did she find it?'

'Perfectly shocking. It was written by a man called Margam—Henry Margam.' Mary looked about her nervously. 'I do hope he isn't here tonight.'

'Your mama would faint away?'

'I am sure she would.'

Bella thought of saying more but smiled and made her excuses. Across the room Cissie Cornford was engaged in explaining to Sir William who he really was, a disconcerting habit she had with everybody new to her acquaintance and one the Cornishman was suffering in spluttering silence.

'I have taken the liberty of inviting my good friend Mr Robert Judd here tonight,' he interrupted in a booming voice. 'I hope you have no objection.'

It took a great deal to stop Lady Cornford in her tracks, but the insolence of treating her home like a public house or wayside inn did for her. She stared at Skillane as though he were the wild man from Borneo. Bella was amused; but when she glanced back at Mary Skillane, she was astonished to see a quite unmistakable look of terror on the girl's face.

There were two or three hackneys waiting in Bayley Street. The first cab on the rank was in the care of a genially tipsy man who stirred up his horse with affectionate words and a light flick of a ribboned whip. Bella sank back against the leather cushions feeling vexed and out of sorts. The interior of the cab stank of men—of pomade, and boot polish and the general whiff of how men smell, even the most particular of them. She drew down the window and stared out at the crowded pavements as they swung very gently downhill towards Trafalgar Square, in convoy with dozens of other cabs.

As happened almost every time she parted from Lady Cornford, she vowed never to go there again. That consummate gossip-monger had mentioned the one name calculated to pierce Bella's heart. If Philip Westland was under one of the top hats bobbing down Charing Cross Road, she would make it her pleasure to jump out and dot his eye. Since the chances of meeting him in this way were slim, she hoped instead it was raining cats and dogs in Vienna or wherever else the secret shadows gathered over good-natured and utterly adorable spies.

CHAPTER THREE

Philip Westland was not of course in Vienna, nor in Constantinople, Kabul or anywhere else exotic, but could be found as large as life in Bella's drawing room, playing boisterous cards with his childhood friend William Kennett. Bella recognised the voices as she took off her velvet cape and examined herself in the entrance hall's gilt-framed mirror. Her hands trembled. Perhaps her eyes sparkled more than they had done for several hours and there was a small blue vein at her throat that she wished would go away. Mrs Venn, her housekeeper, appeared on tiptoe like a servant in a play.

'The gentlemen arrived an hour ago,' she whispered. 'And said they were sure you would be pleased to see them.'

'Thank you, Mrs Venn.'

'I told them you were round at Lady Cornford's,' the housekeeper added with a shy smile, 'and they said they would wait with impatience for your return, Mr Westland looking so bronzed and happy.'

Bella skewered the sentimental Mrs Venn with a glance and, heaving up a nervous sigh, entered her drawing room.

In many other locations across London when men sat down to cards, there was money involved. The game these two played had been invented by Kennett when he was six and they were the only people in the world to understand or tolerate the lack of rules.

21

'Black Dog!' Kennett cried on the turn of a card—and not a black suit either.

'Stay, sir!' Westland cried, flourishing the three of hearts. 'I reply with Byron and again double Byron.'

'That is low of you, Westland.'

They looked up at Bella's entrance, grinning apishly.

'Mrs Wallis,' Kennett rose to greet her.

'How lovely to see you again, Mr Kennett,' Bella replied, extending her hand.

Philip Westland watched her with a half-smile. When she turned to greet him, he pre-empted whatever she might have to say by holding her lightly by her upper arms and planting a kiss on her cheek. The breath of a kiss. 'I have been abroad,' he murmured.

'So I imagined.'

William Kennett watched them with perhaps a little too much interest. He was tall and stick-thin, with a bright buzz of red hair and (Bella judged secretly) a beguiling mouth. As described by Westland, his friend was the cleverest man in England. At his house in Chiswick he had stables crammed to the doors with what he called his bright ideas: at the same time he had never made a single thing that worked.

'You are playing Black Dog, I perceive, Mr Kennett. How does the game end?'

'Oh, I should be mortified to think that it ever could.'

'But, say, if one player loses all his cards?'

'That would be quite terrible.'

'Bella wants to ask you what, then, is the point?' Westland smiled.

'The point?' Kennett frowned. 'A very deep question, one I have trained myself never to ponder. Perhaps it is to involve Westland and nothing more ambitious than that.'

'To divert him, you mean?'

'He has more than enough diversions. A very lazy man altogether. No, I like my verb better, I think.' His smile was humorous but Bella did wonder—and not for the first time—how much Kennett was in love with his friend.

'How did things go at Cissie Cornford's?' Westland asked gently.

Bella shrugged and raised her eyebrows. 'There was a man there tonight called Skillane. A very bumptious old man at that. With rather a lovely daughter.'

To both their amazement, Kennett sat down as if shot. 'I have met Mary Skillane,' he muttered. 'Did she look well?'

'She blushes very prettily.'

Whatever slight tension there had been in the room was dispersed as if by gunshot. Cognac was called for—an astonishing, because unexpected, story was revealed. Kennett was smitten with the girl Bella had dismissed only half an hour ago as a simpering nitwit. They had met at the mathematician Pybus's house in Draycott Gardens.

'You do not know Freddie and Cora Pybus but Philip does. A more rackety household cannot exist in London. Freddie is barely of this world at all and Mrs Pybus—'

'I know her to be a poet,' Bella warned.

'Then you know most of what there is to know. There are five children, all of them as wild as Dartmoor ponies. To make the story short,

23

Adelaide, whose birthday party it was, stepped too close to the fire and her petticoats caught alight.'

Kennett studied Bella carefully. 'Miss Skillane doubtless struck you as idiotic in many respects. She has no conversation and is terrified of her father. But as the child screamed, she seized one end of the cloth covering the table and wrenched it free, scattering I don't know how many plates and cups into the bargain. She wrapped up little Adelaide and while I don't say she saved her life, she prevented serious burns to the child's legs. I have never seen anything finer. Quick, instinctive and completely the right thing.'

'My dear fellow,' Westland murmured.

'She is quite wonderful,' Kennett insisted, as much to himself as to anyone else. 'I am not sure how love strikes in the normal way of things but I must tell you I have not stopped thinking about her since this happened.'

'Have you spoken to her of your feelings?'

'Her father has her virtually under lock and key in Cadogan Square. I sent in my card and had it returned. A letter I wrote to Mary came back to me unopened, delivered by the hand of the butler.'

'There is a butler?'

'Sir William is as mad as a March hare. He has a house in Cornwall not much smaller than St Pancras station.'

'Let me ask you,' Bella said quietly. 'Who is Mr Robert Judd?'

There was a tight silence. 'Was he there tonight?' Kennett asked.

'I left before he arrived. The news of his coming seemed to upset Miss Skillane quite dreadfully.'

'She is promised to him. I shall do everything in

24

my power to make sure he does not get her. Even if I have to kill him.' He stood, trapped by his feelings into a display of trembling Bella had never before seen in him and did not know he was liable to.

'You do not mean that,' she said.

'The man is an out-and-out scoundrel. To him, Mary is no more than an acquisition, like a new carriage or a pair of matched guns. She is a route to her father's wealth, which is enormous. Well, Judd simply shall not have her.' In an absent gesture, he turned over a card and laughed a bleak laugh. 'Look at that, if you will.'

'The seven of clubs,' Bella supplied.

'The Borodino,' Kennett corrected. 'It is a sign, Mrs Wallis. A sure and certain sign. Judd can go fish for her. She is—or perhaps it would be more honest to say—she will be mine.' He rose, tugging haplessly at the wings to his waistcoat. 'I have said too much.'

Westland touched him on the arm. 'If you intend to leave under such a cloud of anger, then please allow me to walk you home.'

'To Chiswick and back? I don't think so.'

'Must you walk at all?' Bella wondered. 'Wouldn't a cab be more convenient?'

'He walks everywhere,' Philip Westland explained.

*   *   *

In Bella's book, asking your occasional lover where he has been for the last three weeks would be very bad form. Asking him if he cared to unmask himself as an international spy was beyond her

25

powers altogether. They lay in bed, holding hands like Hansel and Gretel. Unprompted, Westland gave a very funny account of a hotel in Cognac, without quite saying what he was doing there. Bella resolved not to ask. But love and silence are impossible bedfellows. She listened to Westland's breathing for a while and was relieved when he answered her unspoken question for her.

'I make these continental excursions because if I am not with you—I mean as we are now, tonight—London is intolerable,' he explained.

'It's not for me to ask where you have been.'

'Is it not?'

'Oh, Philip! I'm just happy to have you here now.'

They kissed. Westland smoothed out the neck to her nightgown. 'Did you know I have a sister?'

'I did not.'

'I have a sister eight years younger than me.'

'You have kept her very quiet.'

'She lives in Jarnac, on the banks of the Charente.'

'In a wonderfully elegant chateau?'

'No,' Westland said calmly. 'In an asylum.'

There was much more to say about Sarah Westland—her three attempts at suicide, her helpless indifference to the world outside, the frightening power of her silence—that always reminded Philip of the Alps under snow.

'Philip, I am so sorry to hear this.'

'No one can say whether she is happy. She is calm.'

'Calm is good,' Bella whispered.

'Perhaps. I suppose Cissie Cornford has a much more dramatic explanation for my absences.'

26

'Why do you say that?'

'The only time I met her she assured me that a man we both knew slightly was a spy in the pay of a foreign government.'

Bella sat up in the dark, alarmed. Philip laughed and dragged her down on to his chest. 'He was—he is—a perfectly respectable gentleman farmer from Sussex. His darkest deed, so far as I know, has been to take a party of sporting neighbours to play a fortnight's cricket in Corfu. Lady Cornford saw black iniquity in this. For her it was altogether too innocent an explanation.' Though, he reflected privately, that might be how a very different game was played. It was not much more absurd than buzzing about France like a postman.

Bella sat up again and pulled her gown over her head. She took his arm and drew it across her breast. 'Cissie Cornford is a foolish, interfering old woman.'

*　　　*　　　*

In the morning, Cognac hotels and Charentais asylums were not to be mentioned, any more than steamrollers or porpoises. They took breakfast in companionable silence, Westland reading his *Times* and munching thoughtfully on toast and marmalade. Bella watched him with the greatest affection. If he were a spy—and who would employ such a naturally open and honest man in such work—was it any business of hers, she thought? If she wanted to empty his life of all its secrets, honour demanded she must do the same herself. Meanwhile, the sun winked in the marmalade dish, Philip's newspaper crackled cheerfully, outside the

27

windows Orange Street girded itself for another lazy and indulgent day.

'Would you say all's right with the world?' she asked, drenched from top to toe in happiness.

Philip lowered *The Times* for a moment. 'It says here that the steamer *Berwickshire* has run aground with a cargo of nitrates in Buenos Aires, but in every other respect I would judge we are managing to keep an equilibrium. So, yes, I might go so far as to say that.'

His smile was like a meadowful of birds.

Well, Bella thought, with the faintest touch of guilt, we have left out your friend William Kennett, poor fellow. He must be suffering a shadow or two in Chiswick. But then, that was love's pleasant agony for you. He must fight his own battles. On a day like this she was surely in the right of it: nothing much could go amiss. There were no dragons to slay and the waters of the lake that London sometimes seemed lay placid and undisturbed.

CHAPTER FOUR

Holborn Circus: bathed in sunshine though the day had started out frosty. On the south side lay St Andrew's, a very ancient foundation rebuilt by Sir Christopher Wren. At about ten in the morning, Constable Henry Darby was directed there by a pie-seller with a Christian conscience, a ratty little chap with a tray around his neck and a squared-off paper hat. He accompanied Darby as far as the graveyard and then nodded with his chin.

'Good man,' the policeman grunted. 'I'll have a tuppeny pie off you and then you can scarper.'

Fluttering beside a sixteenth-century vault was what seemed like a black shroud. Dust devils had blown paper and leaves against it. Darby laid down his pie on the tomb of one Cornelius Temminck, took off his helmet and wiped the band with a tobacco-brown handkerchief.

'Now then, Molly,' he said quietly. 'You're a bit out of your road up here. You haven't been sleeping out, I do hope.'

'Molly Clunn,' the fallen figure mumbled, as if answering roll-call.

'I know that, old girl. I know who you are. It's Harry Darby come to see you. Sit up, if you can. I've brought your breakfast.'

Molly Clunn, the music hall darling. Darby had been taken across the river to Lambeth by his uncles to see her perform when he was ten. He'd seen her again the night before his wedding and yet again when Lily was still sucking on her mother's tit. Harry Darby was not the toughest copper in the division but still a hard man, as you had to be to do this job. Accordingly, he managed not to flinch as Molly struggled like a beetle to right herself. He breathed through the nose to minimise the stink of her.

'I'm a goner, Harry.'

'No, you ain't. But you can't lig about this old churchyard, good Lord you can't. And you with no boots on you.'

Molly plucked at her sodden skirts. 'I used to be so particular and that's no lie.'

'You've fallen on hard times. But it's not over for you yet, no, not by a long chalk.'

29

When Molly Clunn smiled her response, he saw that her four top teeth had disappeared. The woman he remembered as plumply seductive in fleshings and a skirt that opened at the front, a red bodice and fake diamonds in her hair was now a hideous scarecrow. Her half-exposed breasts were hardly more than flaps of skin, her shoulders bare to the bone. Old Molly was on her way out.

There was a footfall on the worn Yorkstone pavement and the sexton—if he was a sexton—(Darby was a bit hazy on church authorities but this one wore a cassock cinched with a leather belt with some silly bloody wallet hanging from it)—stood over them both. He was a stout and red-faced man with close-cut silver hair.

'Are you arresting this woman?' he demanded.

'No, sir, I am not.'

'Well, she can't stay here.'

Darby rose and put his helmet back on. That, and the set of his jaw, gave him what he thought of as the full majesty of the law.

'Now you don't want to go interfering with a police officer in the course of his duties.'

The sexton simply stared him down. 'I have taken your number and I want you both out of this yard at once.'

'Or?'

'Or he'll fetch a policeman,' Molly croaked with a cackle that turned into a paroxysm of coughs. In attempting to stand up, she collapsed like a tent whose poles had buckled.

'I will not have begging in the church precincts,' the sexton said. He picked up the pie. 'If this creature is a vagrant, you must apply the law.'

Experience had taught Darby that when it came

30

to the poor, church people could be some of the most vindictive bastards on earth. The man in the cassock was in the way of being a gentleman; at any rate definitely not some shit-shoveller. With such as these, it was best to tread careful. Accordingly, he gave him his slow burn, an unblinking eye contact that did indeed unsettle the sexton.

'The lady is not a vagrant. She is out of her way this morning but her address is known to me.'

'A lady, you call her?'

'Is the vicar on the premises?' Darby decided, tugging down his tunic briskly. 'Because if he is, we shall just walk round there together, you and me.'

'The minister is preparing for matins.'

'Then off we go. Leaving the pie,' he added.

They saw the curate at the church door, a hand-wringing young man with a cruel centre-parting.

'Must there be all this fuss?'

'The lady—what this gentleman has called a creature—is Molly Clunn, once as well-known on the boards as any artiste who ever trod them.'

'But what is she doing in our churchyard, Constable?'

'It is not for me to teach you your duties, sir, but one explanation might be that she has a wish to be nearer to God.'

'What fiddlesticks,' the sexton snorted.

'Well, then,' Darby said. 'If you was to step around the corner with me, Reverend, you might tell her that's not possible. That you would like me to have her took up for trespassing.'

The curate bit his lip, considered, and then nodded. But when they came to the churchyard, Molly had gone.

'Is she a member of our parish?' the curate

asked, uncertainly.

'Is Morton's Yard part of your parish?' Darby countered.

'I—perhaps. I cannot be sure.'

'You have never heard of it?'

'I think not.'

But the sexton knew what this exchange was about. His face softened unexpectedly. Inside the church, the organ began to play and the first of the congregation were arriving. Disraeli had been christened in this church and Hazlitt married from it. That day's churchgoers were correspondingly well-heeled.

The curate's attention was beginning to wander. 'You say she is from Morton's Yard?'

'For a few days longer,' Darby said.

'And then what?'

'That's for you to say, sir. But no longer among us in this vale of tears. And that's no error.'

Darby touched the brim of his helmet and walked off. At the top of Shoe Lane he stopped to look for Molly over the heads of others. He searched to see whether the crowds were parting around some obstruction on the pavement or—as he told his wife that night—whether the Angel of the Lord was hovering. Nothing.

The way to keep your feet from playing merry hell on this job was to wiggle your toes and arch your instep. And, as Darby's sergeant was always reminding him with a good deal of sarcasm, to keep moving. He tucked his thumbs in his belt and began to walk up Holborn, steady as you like, one foot in front of the other, the law in motion.

*   *   *

Bella's office—or more accurately her place of work—lay in Fleur de Lys Court, off the Strand. It was here that she wrote the novels published under the name of Henry Ellis Margam. This nom de plume was very precious to her: not more than a dozen people in London knew Margam's real identity. It was as she wanted it. Though she did not like the fellow—no, not in the slightest—she very much liked being two people at once. There was mischief in it that not even the heady romance with Philip Westland could abate.

Margam was what was called a sensationalist—it was the heated pages of his latest book *The Widow's Secret* that had drawn a blush to Lady Skillane's cheeks, as reported by her daughter Mary. His more sophisticated readers found him alarmingly accurate about people and situations that they knew, or thought they knew. The moral of a Margam novel was not that love triumphs, nor that the meek will inherit the earth. It was that the world was a dangerous place and—once the thin veneer of manners had been stripped from it—unknowable.

There were by now eight such novels. This was not to say very much, for Mrs Toaze-Bonnett, with whom Bella shared a publisher, could write faster than she could knit and was on her thirty-fourth. She often protested to friends that she was sure she had no idea where these innocent tales came from. Bella could have told her: from a dusty and ramshackle barnful of clichés located in the otherwise empty pastures of Mrs Toaze-Bonnett's mind.

A Henry Ellis Margam novel was of a different

33

order altogether. It came from Bella's uneasy sense of how the world really was—that was to say, how reason (and justice) was balanced precariously over an abyss. The trick was not to prate nor wring the hands but to find the story that might illustrate the metaphor. Every Margam novel, wherever it wandered, set out from London, both the view from such as Cissie Cornford's windows and the more brutal, less forgiving city landscapes that lay beyond.

All the same, Bella was enough of a professional to know that happiness was the best pen wiper. It was this that Philip Westland gave her. Genial and good-natured man that he was, he had set off after breakfast for Chiswick. His friend Kennett was working on a steam launch (better to say a clinker-built rowing boat with a furnace and boiler amidships, topped by a seven-foot funnel). It was approaching the day of the vessel's second river trial. On its first outing, the boat had turned turtle.

'It sank under the weight of its own impudence,' Westland confessed. 'But since then he has cannibalised another boat and using the formers and risers from that has added all-important length to the keel. You could say a new seriousness has resulted. True, she is a little by the stern—'

'Westland, do you have the faintest idea what you are talking about?'

'No. But I like him. And admire him.'

'Has he ever been in love before?'

'Oh, love! What's that, dearest Bella? A momentary distraction. Good Lord, we inventors hardly have time for such nonsense. This is the elemental struggle, man against nature.'

But he kissed her lingeringly for all that.

Her pleasure at walking across the mossy paving of Fleur de Lys Court and pushing on the chocolate-brown door proved short-lived. Sitting at the once proud rosewood desk was Captain Quigley, eating a huge slice of veal and ham pie and spearing beetroot with his knife. His greeting was boisterous.

'And didn't I see you with your young man recently in St Martin's Lane?' he crowed.

'The boy you saw was my godson.'

'And every inch the warrior, the little chap! An officer any man would be proud to follow into the jaws of death and the Cape a safer place for his going there, I don't doubt.'

Bella stared in amazement at the entirely self-styled Captain Quigley. 'How did you know he was being sent to the Cape?'

'My dear lady! It is Quigley's business to know any detail touching your well-being. Why else would you employ me?'

'Do I employ you?'

'I think I have offered you some service in the past,' he smirked. 'Now, I have managed to get hold of some of that paper Mr Margam likes so much and also took the liberty of obtaining some of the German nibs he favours. The old office has been swept out, inkwells filled, everything ready for a bout of scribbling, if you are so minded.'

Quigley had a new trick—seething spittle through the gaps in his bottom teeth. He'd seen it done by a lawyer cove and admired it as a piece of punctuation. But he could not completely abandon waggling the eyebrows either. So he seethed and semaphored, his lips reddened by beetroot.

'And what are your plans now?'

35

'Me? I shall step round to the pub for a handy bit of business. Did you know,' he added formally, 'that down there in the Congo the currency of the country is brass stair-rods?'

'And you have some?'

'About four hundred,' Quigley confirmed, sliding out of the door with a final salute.

Bella settled at the rosewood desk with only the most sketchy idea of what she might write. The nibs that Quigley had procured lay nesting in a battered cardboard box. She tipped a few out and fitted one to her favourite holder, an ivory item the Captain had presented her with for the composition of *Deveril's Disgrace*. It was almost certainly stolen; if not, acquired from dubious sources. Bella liked its weary elegance. And at least the ink with which she wrote was honestly acquired, for she bought it herself from a stationer's in Fleet Street. But then this was only after Quigley had tried to persuade her to write in violet ink, of which he had several pint bottles in wicker sleeves, come by in the same way as his four hundred stair-rods.

She had been working no more than a quarter of an hour when Quigley returned. His expression was unusually sombre. 'There is trouble,' he said, wiping his lips with the cuff to his jacket sleeve.

'And what trouble might that be?'

'I've just come across Billy Murch. Who sends his best regards, by the way. But otherwise much broken up.'

All the happiness Bella had felt at breakfast time disappeared in an instant. Murch was a name she recognised with a mixture of pleasure and dread. He had been the model for Meinherzen, the implacable hero of her latest book, *The Widow's Secret*. Even as disguised in the pages of a sensationalist novel, there was much to admire in Billy and not a little to fear. Quigley claimed him as a friend, but the gaunt and lonely figure was about as far removed from him as was a tiger from a tethered goat.

Bella laid down her pen carefully and looked Quigley in the eye. 'You say he is distressed?'

'Drunk, hardly fit to stand, the shakes on him like a wounded beast. He has found, or thinks he has found Molly Clunn,' the Captain nodded.

It took a moment or two for Bella to focus. 'She is in London?'

'You remember her, doubtless.'

Molly Clunn: bold and brash enough for two but reckless with the bottle. There had been loose talk that she and Murch might make a go of things— but all that had come from the Captain, who was of a generally sentimental cast of mind. Bella had met Molly once and once only and saw immediately that the very thing that Quigley admired so much in her and made her right for old Billy—her merriness—would in the end be her undoing. Murch had great qualities but a love of foolishness was not one of them.

Bella searched her memory. The two of them had set up somewhere along the Regent's Canal— a basement room, only to be got at through a thicket of alder. It was dry enough and clean enough but Murch (though he did not say so) detested it. Molly walked out on him a week or so later.

After that, reports of her were scant. She was in Brighton, later on in Portsmouth. She was well, she

37

was ill, she was in the gutter. Some said she was dead of the hard stuff. Murch himself shifted about in this same period, walking to Kent for the hop-picking, working the docks at Ipswich. When he came back to London, he stayed out on the wrong side of the river at Kennington and visited his friend the Captain only seldom. And now this.

'Is she in a bad way?'

'Hard to imagine worse.'

'Can we help?'

'I have sent word to Mr Urmiston, who values Billy highly. Doesn't know the lady but would cross an ocean for dear old Bill. Waiting on him now.'

Pat upon cue, Charles Urmiston arrived from his herbalist shop in Shelton Street, sidling into the office in his usual shy way.

'And if this isn't like old times,' the Captain exclaimed, after pumping his hand. 'Which I shall just run around to Tonio's for a jug of fresh coffee and a handful of biscuits.'

When he had gone, Urmiston smiled at Bella. 'You are looking wonderfully well,' he said softly.

She walked around her desk and kissed him, nuzzled her head in the crook of his neck and huddled him to her. There was a time in his life when Urmiston himself had been a sort of floating wreck. Bella had rescued him from the misery of losing his wife and then stood by astonished as he found what proved to be the true love of his life, the incomparable Mrs Bardsoe. In latter months she had seen him seldom and the role his commonsense had played in her judgement of what was right had passed to Philip Westland.

Comparison between the two men was inevitable. There never had been a romantic attachment with Urmiston, however, and while she admired him, she fancied she could never need him, not in the way she needed Philip. All that said, she was surprised how the snuff of his woolly collar, the familiar stoop to his back and gangling wrists made her eyes prick.

'How I have missed you,' she whispered.

Urmiston chuckled gently. 'We hardly live a mile apart, dearest Bella,' he chided. 'I should add that Hannah sends her love.'

They disengaged, each of them feeling a little foolish.

'This sounds a bad business,' Bella said to ease the moment.

'I fear the worst. We don't even know for sure where Molly is, exactly. But deep in some hellish slum.'

'Have you seen Mr Murch?'

'He took a bite with us at Shelton Street last night. He looked terrible, Bella. I have never seen a man so distraught. He blames himself for what has happened to Molly. He does not say so but I can see it in his eyes.'

'But he was under no formal obligation to her, surely?'

Urmiston shook his head gently. 'Once upon a time I would have agreed with you: he owes her nothing. But it doesn't work like that in Billy's world. She loved him and he let her down.'

Bella could not hold back a shudder. Urmiston, who had once been of her own class, had crossed a boundary and now lived far closer to that other, turbulent London she herself only visited. Molly's story was in its way the basis for a Margam plot: a woman loves a man who does not want her and as a consequence is flung into the pit. But Henry Ellis Margam's world was of dinner parties, white gloves and letters it might have been more sensible never to have sent. Bella's shudder came from having to acknowledge the basic emptiness of popular fiction.

'That poor woman,' she heard herself mutter.

'I have put myself at Murch's service for any rescue operation, which he has made clear is dangerous, very dangerous work.'

'I will come with you,' Bella said at once.

'No. That is gracious but it will not do.'

'I am not trying to be gracious. She will need a woman by her.'

Urmiston shook his head. 'That simply cannot happen. This is entirely man's work.'

'You do talk such piffle sometimes, Charles.'

He shrugged but did nothing to alter his expression, which was grave and—around the normally kindly blue eyes—a little bit fearful.

And shamefully, Bella herself was uneasy. Not because she was afraid, but rather that her alter ego, Henry Ellis Margam, whom she was hoping to encourage to enter the office and hang his hat, had turned at the threshold and disappeared. Evanesced. He was a man who preferred to stay on the sandy paths, among the parasols. He had told Bella many times that she was armed against life with nothing more than a pen and superb grey eyes. Mischief, to Henry Ellis Margam, was a monogrammed handkerchief found under the bed; or a cache of love letters hidden in the boathouse. Anything else was utter madness. There was enough folly in a misplaced lock of hair to furnish any novel with its plot.

CHAPTER FIVE

Quigley came back with his can of coffee and the three of them sat uncomfortably either side of Bella's desk, debating what to do. The Captain, like Urmiston, saw the search for Molly Clunn in expeditionary terms. It suited his nature to bluster and he tried to make clear that no African exploration could be more fraught than what he had in mind.

Quite suddenly, Philip Westland arrived, as if from a different story altogether. Even his clothes marked him apart: he wore a cream linen suit and a soft shirt, which were not in themselves so very extraordinary but had (in the perpetual gloom of Fleur de Lys Court) some of the effect of fancy dress. He shook hands with Urmiston and the Captain, stood about for a few uncomfortable minutes and then whisked Bella away to lunch at Fracatelli's.

He grasped at once that he had walked into some piece of business that was none of his own. That much he could see in Bella's uneasy smile and only half-effected introductions. But he knew she had an almost superstitious reverence for the Strand restaurant with its snowy white tablecloths and crystal chandeliers.

Fracatelli himself seated them and flourished the wine list. 'We don't see you often enough, Mrs Wallis,' he protested, eyeing Philip surreptitiously at the same time.

'This is a very amiable place,' Westland said after he had gone. 'Are those gentlemen lawyers over there?'

Bella's glance towards the table he indicated with his chin was cursory. She found her hands were trembling. 'I was very surprised to see you, Philip. I thought you were over at Chiswick for the day.'

'As did I. But it seems there was a faint chance of Kennett meeting Miss Skillane at the Royal Academy and all other business was suspended. We came back into the West End together. Mrs Venn told me where I might find you.'

'And what did you make of Fleur de Lys Court?'

Philip examined his napkin before pulling it through its mahogany ring. 'Must I say?'

'Of course! Else why would I ask you?'

'This then: I was greatly startled.'

'I find it suits very well,' Bella said, brusquely.

'You mean, perhaps it suits Mr Henry Ellis Margam. About that, I can't comment.'

'That is true,' she snapped.

'But of course, in this instance, it is not he who is going to suffer if things go wrong.'

And that was it: even in such a brief and apparently casual visit to Fleur de Lys Court, he had learned enough to know what she was planning for that night. Not in any detail, she was sure of that, but either Urmiston or Quigley had said a word or two too many.

On a childlike impulse, she pushed away her plate. 'I cannot stay,' she decided.

Philip studied her without expression. 'Of course you can,' he said in a steady and emotionally neutral tone. 'I have no right to insist, but—' and at last he smiled briefly '—I must.'

And when she looked suitably crestfallen, his

42

smile became a soft and indulgent laugh. He covered her hand with his. 'Be easy, Bella. We are not quarrelling. We are merely two people taking lunch.'

She stayed; and for four courses and a very good bottle of Barolo he entertained her across a range of subjects, including a very scandalous account of how belly-dancing worked, or, perhaps more accurately, the amount of flesh it set in motion. That night's expedition to retrieve Molly Clunn was never mentioned once. They parted on the pavement outside, just as if things were as he had said they were—two close friends concluding a pleasant lunch. But then, at the last moment, Westland touched her sleeve. In fiction, squires' daughters came close to fainting when this happened, generally at the lynchgate when Captain Brooke looked into their eyes. Bella felt the same giddy sensations.

'The thing of it is,' Philip said gently, 'I had no right to spring myself upon you earlier. And certainly, dearest Bella, I had no idea what I might find. Without wishing to, I overstepped the mark.'

She stared after him as he sauntered away, holding his hat in his hand, arms swinging. Characteristically, he did not look back.

But then she knew him well enough to see that he had delivered, in his own inimitable fashion, a warning and a rebuke. Fleur de Lys Court was the door into a world he would far rather she did not enter.

*   *   *

Quigley insisted upon taking a gun, a French

cavalry pistol with a dangerously weak breech. Urmiston was given a sawn-down pick handle—shortened so that it could be hidden in a sleeve and dropped out at a moment's notice, a trick he had tried repeatedly but could not master. He discarded Quigley's idea and went for a walk, coming back with a muddy stave from a building site.

The Captain did not want Bella Wallis to accompany the party, no, not for love nor money—but if she was going to be pigheaded about it, better she dressed accordingly. My word, yes.

Bella went to Shelton Street and consulted Urmiston's beloved, Hannah Bardsoe, as to what this might mean in a practical sense. That plump and good-natured woman ignored the question and begged her fervently not to go at all. 'The Captain is in the right of it for once. Leave it to him, as he is used to the perils of the underworld, tub of lard though he may be.'

'We're hardly going to the Congo, Mrs Bardsoe. And Charles will take care of me.'

'Charles? He cannot look after himself in even the smallest shower of rain,' Hannah cried. 'I know it has to be done but I will tell you straight: I'm afeared for the lot of you.'

'Tell me what I must do to disguise myself.'

'No perfume, not a hint of soap, no pins or brooches, combs or anything of the kind. No corsets nor stockings. Nothing in short that would make you a woman at all in the wider world. You go as an animal, Mrs Wallis, a brute thing.'

'You are not overegging the pudding somewhat?'

Hannah Bardsoe stood, distracted. 'My dear,'

44

she said with great simplicity, 'you can have no idea.'

'Will you go with me to Coleman's, to help me choose some clothes?'

They walked to the end of Shelton Street and turned in at a stub of a passage where Ma Coleman kept her old clothes shop. At the bottom of this tiny cul-de-sac was a timbered Jacobean house bleached silver. Time had almost collapsed it: the structure leaned drunkenly against the blank brick walls of its neighbours. Ma had it for her warehouse, though it would have been risking death to move any higher than the ground floor. The door and windows had long gone and an acid stench came from the mountains of cast-off clothing that filled the property front to back. Death and destitution spoke to Bella from this hideous storehouse.

Ma had the knack of silence. Her face was filthy and her hands blackened, but she had intelligent eyes. She sorted her stock with a long pole, dragging this and that out on to the ruined pavement without comment. Bella found she could not so much as touch anything and so the choice was made by Hannah Bardsoe: a once white shawl, two torn chemises, a black tent of a dress in the cheapest cotton.

'Boots?' Ma asked, pointing with her pole to a cascade of them.

'No,' Bella said at once. Hannah laid a reassuring hand on her arm.

'Now for these old rags, Ma,' she said, 'if they are worth more than a few pence apiece, you can have 'em back without putting yourself to the trouble of searching out more.'

45

'This ain't no charity.'

'It ain't no emporium neither.'

The clothes were carried back to the little shop in Shelton Street and boiled up in the washer, then flogged in the tiny yard. Hannah examined every seam for lice, finding a few left alive and cracking them with her thumbnail.

'When do you go?'

'Quigley says tonight, as soon as it is dark.'

'Then you shall stop here and eat with us. These rags can go round to the bakehouse to be dried and then we shall see.'

*   *   *

London had grown heavy with the threat of summer storm. Cutting through its everyday smells—smoke, horse piss, dust, soot, pollen— many could identify the whiff of imminent electrical discharge. Ladies in Belgravia felt the sharp stab of unwonted headaches: across the river in Lambeth, round-shouldered men stood out of doors with their hands in their pockets, wondering at the lack of light. It was said that at Epping the storm had already arrived and that the great forests were on fire in several places. At their northern edge, the oak before the Woodbine Inn had been struck by lightning, killing two labourers sheltering under it. An oak is only an oak but this one was famous for having shaded the brow of the great Wesley.

But in central London it was eerily still. Many who had cause to cross the Thames during the late afternoon remarked on the river's unnatural colour.

Captain Quigley and Charles Urmiston stood outside the shop in Shelton Street, feeling the sky press down on them. What they could see of it was almost all black.

'You are very calm, Captain.'

'What it is, I am heartbroke. A man makes only a few pals of the true blue kind in his lifetime.'

'You knew her that well?'

'You should have seen her when she was young.'

'And Mr Murch—Billy? Did he know her when she was young?'

'Not so much.'

'Where is he now?'

'We meet at the bottom of Fetter Lane, as soon as it has come full dark.'

Bella joined them, her hair undone and artful smudges of soot on her cheeks and throat. The black dress hung open a little, revealing the slope to a far too white breast.

'No,' Quigley said gently. 'Will you go back inside and have Hannah decorate you with a little more dust?'

But in that instant the storm broke and in seconds they were drenched. They ran indoors and drank a full measure of rum each and shared the last cheroot from Urmiston's paper packet. Then, watched by a fearful Mrs Bardsoe, they hunched their shoulders and set off down the street. As Bella had seen done—but only ever at a distance—she linked arms with the two men and wore the white shawl over her head.

*   *   *

Murch was waiting for them, looming out of the

47

dark, water streaming from a canvas jacket. When he saw Bella, he let out a stifled animal cry.

'The lady is to go back,' he commanded. 'I can't be responsible for her.'

'Listen to me, Billy—' Bella began.

He brushed her words away, white ridges high on his cheeks. 'I cannot have it.'

'She has come to help,' Urmiston said.

Murch stared at them all in turn, as if examining madmen. 'Maybe I should do this on my own,' he muttered.

'Well, you ain't going to, so lead on, Billy boy,' Captain Quigley said through chattering teeth. 'Let's get it done.'

Murch turned on his heel and marched up Fetter Lane. Water ran down the roadway like a black river. The others hurried to keep up. After only a hundred yards, Billy stopped. He pointed into the murk.

'Where we go now is as dangerous a place as any in London. You do exactly as I say. And mark me, Mr Urmiston: if you have to run, you retrace your steps and you run until your heart is fit to burst. Taking the lady with you. Understood?'

'Yes,' Urmiston said, his voice shaking.

'Then this way and God help us all.'

They felt their way into as evil a place as existed in all London. At the top of Morton's Yard a huge mound of dust and cinders had been reduced to a midden—mud and filth spread more than a foot deep across the cobbles. On the far side of this barrier the lights of a pub blinked wanly. A crowd of about thirty milled outside, roaring on the dance of two naked children, their scrawny limbs jerking, their feet splashing in the puddles. Dogs leaped at

48

their heels. There was fiddle music from a hunchback man hardly taller than the dancers.

Murch held them back. 'Wait here,' he ordered in a low voice. 'And you, Mr Urmiston, put your arm around the woman we have with us. Hold that pacifier across your chest, ready for use. The Captain to come with me.'

Urmiston nodded and drew Bella under his arm. The stave he had found for himself was held tight in his hand. The two shrank back against a wall. Murch and Quigley pushed their way into the packed pub and were quickly lost to view.

'This is vile,' Bella whispered. 'I have never been so afraid.'

'Your hands are frozen.'

'From horror. We have done this badly. We must come back by day with half a dozen hired bullies.'

She screamed as an elderly man was pushed against her by the crowd.

He looked up into her face and gaped. 'Mrs Wallis,' he exclaimed, incredulous. 'Penwith, madam. I was in service to Lord Liddiment in better times. You don't remember me? I was under-butler to his lordship at the London house.'

'Mr Penwith!'

The old man put his fingers to his lips in agonised warning. 'Just Penwith. Old Pen, they call me here.'

'But—'

'You are going to ask what I'm doing in this horrible place. Starving, is the answer to that. Dying, the answer to that.'

Bella found that she was clutching both his hands in hers. 'But what has brought you so low?'

'Old age,' he whispered tearfully. 'And want of a

house.'

'Lord Liddiment could do nothing for you?'

'I was turned off at a morning's notice. That was four years ago. His lordship was in Ireland. I doubt he ever knew or noticed.'

They were interrupted by a taller man who lunged at them, his expression wild with drink. 'Now, Pen, who's the judy with the lovely titties?'

'My daughter, Maggsy.'

'Your daughter, my eye.'

Urmiston seemed as if roused from sleep. He stepped between them, the stave in both hands. 'Enough of that.'

'Maggsy, he means no harm,' Penwith pleaded swiftly.

'Means no harm?' Urmiston laughed. 'I'd kill him as soon as look at him.'

But it was Bella who knocked the knife from Maggsy's hand and Bella who swung her forearm against his throat. The crowd that had been watching the naked urchins at once swung round to follow a more interesting story. The man called Maggsy was on his hands and knees and getting ready to spring. As he raised his head, Urmiston leaned into the stroke and drove through the covers as he had once been taught by the school professional, Henry Pye. Plenty of wrist, the bat angled downwards. There was a wet thud. Blood from Maggsy's nose wriggled away like worms in the downpour.

'Finish him!' a woman shrieked. 'Go on, bust him up!'

Her companion was already kneeling by the body, her hands plunging into his trouser pockets.

'We're looking for a friend of ours,' Bella

shouted. 'And want no trouble.'

Murch was back by her side, his fingers closed like a vice over her elbow. 'Don't speak,' he growled. 'Not a word more. Walk away slow. Perce, take her other side. Don't strut, for all love. Saunter.'

'You should have finished him, mister,' one of the naked children advised Urmiston. She hopped from foot to foot, shivering, her arms crossed over her chest. 'You let him off light. And now he'll have you, you see if he don't.'

'Is the white-haired old cove still with us?' Quigley whispered, groping for Penwith. 'Step ahead of us, dad, and lead the way. It's as black as a cow's insides down the lane here.'

'Where are we going?'

'Randall's,' Murch replied. 'You may know the house.'

*   *   *

There was no problem with rights of entry. The front door had long gone and by what tiny light there was Bella could see that so had the ground-floor windows. They were replaced by pennons of sacking blowing wildly in the tempest that had begun to rage. She held on to Urmiston's coat-tails and shuffled into a narrow hallway hardly less wet than the pavement outside. Her foot touched a sodden bundle. To her horror, it moved: inside the foul wrapping lay a child. Bella reached out with her hand anywhere and found Penwith's bony grasp.

'Breathe through your nose, madam,' he whispered, in the same tone he had once used

51

when accepting her umbrella in Lord Liddiment's marble hallway.

There was a low curse from Billy Murch as his fifth match refused to flare; and then came a pale dish of light from the bulls-eye lantern he had carried hidden in his clothes. A gift from Constable Darby, not to be lost, not to be damaged; to be returned anonymous-like to the steps of the St Bride's nick by midnight sharp and no messing. Darby himself too bloody fly to put his nose anywhere near Morton's Yard, no, not for a sergeant's stripes.

From the back of the house a giant of a man reeled, if giants are measured by height. This one wore a whaler's cap with flaps and a ragged coachman's cape. 'Not here, you don't. You don't come in here, you sorry sacks of shit. Not 'less I see some coin in your hand, you don't.'

There was a sudden sharp coughing sound and he sank unexpectedly to his knees.

'What it is,' Billy Murch said in a low and seemingly reasonable voice, 'I will reach down your throat and rip your lungs out so soon as debate you. I will have your eyes out with these here thumbs, d'you follow me? Well, do you?'

'I am the lodging house keeper,' the giant whined. 'I have my orders.'

'See, but these are your new orders. You make one more peep and I'll finish you, so help me. I will break every fucking bone in your body.'

'She said you might come. She said one day you might come.'

Billy's piteous howl was like an animal's.

*   *   *

52

Molly Clunn had died that afternoon but already the rats had been at her. There were seven other people in the attic room where she lay. In the whole building there were forty more, all of them seemingly struck down by the same mystery illness, a sleeping sickness imported from some mangrove swamp or jungle floor. But it was much simpler than that: they were starving.

Old Pen held Bella back with trembling hands. 'She was ill when she came,' he whispered. 'I spoke to her a few times. A servant of yours maybe?'

'A friend. In her own way, a friend.'

'Now listen, old-timer,' Murch said in a thick voice. 'We cannot move her tonight. But if I was to give you a few coins, could you sit with her and see her took from this rathole in the morning so's we can bury her in the Christian way of things?'

Penwith stared. Murch reached in and dragged him forward by his lapels, his teeth bared. Urmiston, gentle Urmiston, brushed his hands away.

'Can you at least,' he amplified, 'have her taken from here to a place we will designate in the Farringdon Road where we might meet you with better arrangements—a hearse?'

The old man peered at them one by one. 'Tomorrow?'

'At eleven tomorrow.'

'And now,' Quigley added, 'we want a way out of this here attic such as will give us no trouble.'

But it was too late for that. Maggsy and his cronies were pounding up the stairs. Quigley took out the horse pistol and steadied it in both hands, before pointing it down into the dark. When he

53

pulled the trigger, the breech blew off, whistling past his face and killing Penwith instantly. The firing pin had done its work, however, and though the bullet was travelling slow, it found the softest part of Maggsy's face, entering his enraged eye as sweetly as a masonry bee finds the one unmortared crack in a blank wall.

'Up on to the roof,' Murch shouted. 'Quigley to lead the way, the lady to follow. Mr Urmiston to stay with me. And make it quick.'

Bella held on to the tail of the Captain's jacket, shuddering to feel rats run across her feet. A child loomed for an instant and was knocked over. She supposed they would make their escape by skylight, but Quigley dragged her into an attic where the roof had collapsed. The same child they had knocked down took her hand.

'No mistakes now,' Quigley growled. 'One false move out on them tiles and you're a goner. Get up on the ridge. Straddle it and wait for the rest of us.'

'It ain't so hard,' the child boasted. 'Do it all the time. You can get to Creely's, what has a flat roof. T'aint no further than you can spit.'

'Come with me.'

'Not likely,' her guide cackled, disengaging her hand. In another second he had disappeared.

Bella and Captain Quigley clawed their way up the ruined section of roof and on to the ridge.

'To the right, to the right,' Quigley bellowed over the thunder.

'What about the other two?'

'Don't you worry about them.'

Illuminated by acid blue lightning, the dome of St Paul's seemed for a moment to be swimming towards Bella, as if to swallow all this misery like a whale in the ocean or better still (she thought hysterically) shaped like the shadow of God Himself.

*   *   *

Mrs Bardsoe had no tweezers but heated a needle over a candle, her left hand taking a firm grip of Bella's thigh. The men were downstairs, shaking the water out of their hair and clothes like rats.

'Now you can stop that sobbing,' Hannah Bardsoe said, 'for it is nothing but a jag of old wood that—'

Her breath fanned Bella's naked flesh and she grunted once or twice in concentration. 'You've had a night of it and no mistake. But now you're safe and—ah now! Out she comes, as sweet as a nut. A spell the size of my finger! Disinfectant for that and then a light bandage, I think. As for the bruises, why, arnica every time.'

She looked up past Bella's stomach and smiled. 'I'd be obliged for a pull-up, which my knees are creaking like some old gate.'

Bella obliged; and once she had Hannah upright, embraced her and kissed her hair. 'Is there a woman in the world more sensible than you?'

'None,' Hannah agreed. 'After a dab of lye and your bandage, on with your clothes and we'll step downstairs for a spot of refreshment. Unless I mistake, that is Mr Westland's manly voice mingling with the others.'

'How on earth did he get here?'

'Urmiston took the liberty of sending for him. And who give you these bruises on your lovely arm?'

'I'm afraid it was Billy Murch,' Bella replied.

'He's took it very bad, the poor devil. He'll stop with us tonight. And I do hope for long after that. Now listen to me, my dear. Let him and Percy Quigley arrange what is to be done. No more adventures.'

And reaching on tiptoe, she kissed Bella's trembling eyelids.

*   *   *

That night, in the dark of the Orange Street bedroom, she lay on her back like an exhausted swimmer, her arm trapped under Philip's head, his cheek against her shoulder. The rain hammered against the window panes and somewhere a gutter was overflowing, the cascade striking the pavement with a vaguely threatening force.

He knows so much, he has done this before, she thought. Some woman he has never mentioned and never will has taught him how patience unties the tricky knot. She wiped her damp skin with the flat of her hand and pulled her hair away from her face. She thought he was asleep, but his own hand came up and caught her by the wrist.

'It will not do, Bella,' he muttered. 'No more of this.'

For a terrible second she thought he meant the frenzy with which she had made love but of course his mind was on what had passed at Morton's Yard. In daylight, at the breakfast table, she would have been swift to contradict him, for squabbling like children was one of their most intimate activities.

'My arm has gone numb,' she whispered.

Westland raised his head and freed her, before flopping back on to the pillow, sending a puff of lavender-scented air into her mouth.

'Say you love me,' she begged.

'There is nothing of me, not one atom, that does not. But no more adventures. No more reckless journeys to the interior.'

CHAPTER SIX

Before the breakfast table had been laid in Orange Street, before even the curtains had been drawn back, Billy and Captain Quigley, along with another four men they had mustered from among their friends, returned to Morton's Yard and retrieved the bodies of Molly Clunn and Edgar Penwith. The third corpse, that of Maggsy, was nowhere to be seen, though a fourth and fifth— skeletal figures that had died in the night—had been thrown face-down in the mud, where they formed little sodden islands. There was not one dry foot of Morton's Yard from end to end—what was not mud was black water. The place was eerily quiet. Only one person was about, a child in a rag of a dress, cranking the handle to a cast-iron water pump.

Quigley had only once before seen anything to match this desolation: at a train wreck in Kent, where silence had screamed and even the morning air had, it seemed, been sucked out of the sky. Though too small a child to speak, he had had the feeling that something essential, some comforting ordinariness, had been stripped from the world and nothing put in its place. Bodies from the train lay scattered down an embankment—including those of his mother and father—and the engine's boiler was still venting steam. Three of the five carriages had overturned, as if to draw urgent attention to the scene. Yet the overwhelming sense was of an ancient and aboriginal emptiness. And so it was now, at dawn in Morton's Yard.

Bella Wallis had a phrase she had once used against the Captain: for him, thinking was like trying to come it the toff in a duchess's house, tripping on the top step of her stairs and falling all the way to the cellars. This otherwise incurably facetious man sat down wearily on a worn stone, his head in his hands. It is true, he thought, I don't have the words. But if that child at the pump comes across to beg from me, I will kill her.

'Shift yourself, Perce,' said a quiet voice at his back.

It was Murch, bearing Molly's body in his arms. Both corpses were transferred quietly by closed van to a funeral parlour in Portugal Street run by a Mr Mustoe. There they were met by Urmiston, shaved, bathed and in his best suit. It was his job to persuade young Mr Mustoe what was to be done. To smooth over any questions, he carried a small doctor's bag, inside which was a cash box.

'Don't have nothing to do with the old man, he's a bit slow on the uptake these days,' Quigley warned, just before he lifted the door knocker. 'You deal with the boy. They call him Frank. And tell him that for Molly we want the glass hearse.'

For someone who had been roused from his bed at six in the morning by a stranger on the doorstep with two mutilated bodies wrapped in calico, Frank

Mustoe displayed great sang-froid. As would follow from any acquaintanceship with the likes of Quigley, he was deft in asking only the question that mattered—that is to say, where the money was to come from. Urmiston passed him the leather bag. The first of the bodies he looked at was Mr Penwith's and, though he shook his head slightly at the ruined jaw and cheek, he made no comment. But when he looked into Molly's ravaged face, his response astonished Charles Urmiston.

'Poor old girl,' he muttered. Old Mustoe had appeared at the door of the office in his nightshirt. 'See who it is, dad.'

The old man peered, nodded, scratched his armpit and withdrew without a word.

The content of the cashier's box was examined and found agreeable. It was arranged that two professional mourners would walk in front of Molly's hearse, their top hats decorated with black crepe bands reaching halfway down their backs. The horses' bridles would be topped by plumes of black feathers.

'It will all be done according,' Frank Mustoe promised. 'I recognise the lady and I understand the interest that will be shown at her passing.'

'Do you say so?' Urmiston asked, faintly bewildered.

'Molly Clunn's a name that's not forgotten by many a Londoner. I don't want to teach you your grieving, Mr Urmiston, but so soon as you have a date for the funeral, you might wish to invite those as wish to pay their respects but cannot attend the church in person to send their carriages along. Even two or three empty carriages behind the hearse make a show, my word they do.'

'Do you happen to know someone called Captain Quigley?' Urmiston asked.

Mustoe's professional gravity cracked open in a smile. 'Percy Quigley? He sent you, did he? Hiding round the corner, is he? Him and the old dad had a falling out more than twenty years ago, but yes, I know the Captain. Tell him I will step down to Fleur de Lys Court later on this morning. And let him be ready with a list of the nobs that remember her fondly.'

Young Mustoe, who was forty if he was a day, laid his hand along Urmiston's sleeve. His voice was kindly. 'I've seen Molly out and about a few times recent and she deserved a better end. But it is our job to send her to meet her Maker with dignity and—if I may say so—a bit of joy. Yes, those are my words, Mr Urmiston: a bit of joy. Praise we the Lord, as the hymn has it. You have come to the right place.'

*   *   *

Bella had a small space permanently set aside in the morning room of the house in Orange Street. The plain oak desk with locking drawers that stood against one wall was used solely for the final draft of the Margam novels. Mrs Venn, who had a penchant for decorating the rest of the house with cut flowers or bowls of fruit, knew there was never to be anything on this desk but a brass inkstand and a Lyme Regis trilobite Bella used as a paperweight. The desk itself was to be dusted but never polished. Moreover, once seated behind it, her mistress was not to be interrupted by anybody.

All visitors to the house were to be turned away and no letters brought in.

The morning after the disastrous Holborn expedition, Bella set herself up there and for a day and a half sat with a pen in her hand, perfectly ready to write, wanting to write, but paralysed by misery. Philip had left her a gently worded note to say that he would be away for a day or two, and this she interpreted (correctly) as an example of his tact.

Bella had once been told by someone she loved that she was at heart a moralist. The remark was meant to point to the essential seriousness of the Henry Ellis Margam books. The heroes and heroines of the stories stood aghast as they were drawn deeper and deeper into the maze created by the lust and greed of others. The trick of the thing was to make the idea of good seem natural and even commonplace. In Bella's world, choosing right over wrong was as necessary to life as breathing.

And yet Philip Westland's warning had touched a nerve: there was only so far one could go along the path into the horrors of the world. A fog hung permanently over that labyrinth and at some point even the most courageous adventurer faltered. There in the dark, like a canker, lay the multiplying evil of places like Morton's Yard. Bella had stumbled almost to the centre of it and it had left her struck dumb.

When at last her pen began to move, she found she was describing the sun bursting through elms into a broad and empty field. She could not explain to herself why this particular image surfaced rather than the terrors she had so recently experienced.

The memory came from her childhood: she was a six-year-old girl in a white smock and frilled pantaloons, sitting in a bank of buttercups, singing. Even the slight elevation the slope afforded gave her a view across the river to Chelsea, interrupted by the red sails of brick barges sailing upstream.

It is, her father seemed to say to her from beyond the grave, because you were alone in this landscape. That is why you remember it now. The house we lived in was not far away—it was along by the river—but this empty field was like another country, the first frontier you ever crossed. Can you remember what you were singing?

It was a characteristically wry touch. Henry Curtis had died when Bella was twelve and she remembered him most for his clumsy good nature and dry manners. From time to time, as now, he spoke to her as he was in life, a disappointed second son with a houseful of books and just enough invested wealth to live comfortably without the need to work.

'What should I have done?'

She spoke the question aloud. A startled Mrs Venn poked her head around the door.

'Did you ask for something?' she said in her most timid voice. Bella flung down her pen, greatly relieving her housekeeper, who had been going about the house on tiptoe all morning.

'I was calling for a pot of coffee, Mrs Venn. I have been away, I know, and now I am back.'

'Nothing could be more welcome,' Mrs Venn cried joyfully, as if welcoming her mistress home from a long voyage.

*   *   *

Three days later, Molly Clunn was interred in St Anne's, Wardour Street. Over two hundred mourners from the world of the music halls attended the service, many of them dressed in stage costume. Frank Mustoe had been right: eight carriages followed the hearse, their roofs banked with flowers.

Bella missed the service and the ensuing wake: she was seeing Mr Penwith buried in St Dunstan's in the West, a funeral attended by only two other mourners, one of them the former under-butler's distraught employer, Lord Liddiment. 'I might have helped, had I known. We have cottages, here and in Ireland: he would have been welcome to one. It shames me to say I never asked after him and now it has come to this. It is a black day, a bitter black day.'

Following Molly's funeral, Murch stayed the night with Urmiston and Hannah Bardsoe. He walked out without a word early the next morning. Quigley went down into Kent to look for him and was presently sleuthing, as he called it, in Gravesend. He sent a card to Orange Street, saying 'Wild Goose Chase'. There was no signature.

In the same post, a much fuller letter came from Bella's former companion, Marie Claude D'Anville. The Frenchwoman had fled, first to France and then back across the Channel to Worthing. Her new soulmate was a teacher called Iris Burton; they had taken to wearing identical clothes and had scandalised their Sussex neighbours by painting the interior walls of their little villa midnight blue. According to Marie Claude, this colour created an atmosphere of preternatural calm, though she was honest enough to add that the rooms could be gloomy during the hours of daylight. At night and in bed it was like being becalmed in the Pacific Ocean. Candles gave the appearance of watching Polynesian gods.

'She is very young,' Bella explained to Mary Skillane as they sat sipping sherry in Orange Street a few Sundays later. It was midday and the air was heavy with the sound of bells. Bella detested sherry but it seemed to be the only drink Miss Skillane had heard of. She held her glass pinched up in both hands, one at the stem, as though fearing the crystal might shatter. Or that her father might suddenly burst through the door like a rampaging bison.

'You don't worry about her?' she asked of Marie Claude.

'Never. I have not yet met Miss Burton and I worry for her sometimes,' Bella murmured. 'Her new companion can be excessively demanding.'

'Do they live together as man and wife?' Mary whispered, scandalised.

Bella remembered her former lover with the greatest fondness, even to the point of missing her touch once in a while, the scent of her body and her ridiculous neediness.

'Marie Claude would make a very unimpressive husband and an even worse wife. I would say the interests they share can be more poetically expressed.'

'Would I like her?'

Bella considered. 'If you like bedraggled birds of paradise,' she suggested.

But irony formed no part of Mary's experience. Nor was she amused by William Kennett's

64

misadventures with the steam launch he was attempting to build. 'My father is a shipowner and knows the power of the sea. I wonder at Mr Kennett's foolhardiness.'

'Although of course this latest shipwreck took place not far from the Mortlake Brewery. But you must tell him what you feel to his face. He is expected shortly.'

The girl jumped up. 'He is coming here?' she wailed.

Bella laughed and drew her down again. 'You meet under perfectly respectable circumstances.'

'You will say nothing to suggest that I have been critical of his boat-building?'

And this, Bella thought, is love. Miss Skillane was thrilled and wretched all at the same moment, a vein in her throat throbbing, her hands shaking so badly that she actually tucked them under her thighs, like a schoolgirl.

'He comes to lunch. I hope you will join us.'

'Oh, I should like nothing better!'

'Later, you might ask him to escort you around a room or two of the National Gallery.'

'Is he artistic?' the girl cried in dismay.

'About as much as the average cab-horse. But he likes you very much, Mary. I am sure you have noticed. Talk to him about Cornwall. It's my impression that Mr Kennett will hang on your every word.'

'And now you are teasing me.'

For so it seemed when Kennett pitched up. He acted dumbstruck and sat down next to Mary, turning an apple over and over in his hand, one that he had plucked from a bowl of fruit in front of him. Bella indicated to Philip Westland that they

65

should leave the two lovers alone for a few minutes. By way of an excuse, they sauntered up to Leicester Square together. Westland stopped before a familiar presence, the hurdy-gurdy man in his greasy soldier's Glengarry and paid him sixpence to give a turn or two outside the house in Orange Street.

'What does your chum Kennett make of us?' Bella asked.

'Us? There is an us?'

'In my mind there is an us.'

'He thinks me the luckiest man in the world.'

'As indeed you are.'

'And has offered me rather a pretty house he owns in Wiltshire. Village life, Bella. Big skies. A trout stream, I think. Cows and so forth. He describes it all as a writer's paradise.'

Bella seized his hand for a moment. Westland drew it to his lips. 'I told him you were perfectly happy where you were.'

'You understand, Philip?'

'Not for one moment, no. For example, shall you be Mr Henry Ellis Margam forever, do you think? I can quite see how that inkstained scoundrel will never be the man to be solaced by choral evensong in a Wiltshire village. But you and I might teach ourselves such an easy obedience, don't you think?'

'I am a Londoner,' she smiled ruefully. 'There must come an end to it one day—but not yet. Meanwhile, and in so far as I have a heart at all, it is yours.'

Walking back arm in arm, she thought about what she had said, or the part that had touched on London. To leave it would be the same as

66

forsaking a library—a very mixed collection, to be sure, but alive in the way all books are. This sunlight they were bathed in, for example. In the city, sunshine was to be greeted with almost an apologetic grin, as if stolen from elsewhere. Who in Wiltshire gave it so much as a second thought? Bella laughed out loud and reached on tiptoe to kiss Philip Westland's cheek. When he glanced at her enquiringly for the reason, she pointed to a cat yawning in a doorway, its fur coated in dust. Next to the cat was old Abrams and his tray of ribbons and laces. He too was taking the sun while it lasted, his legs stretched out straight in front of him. The uppers to his boots had parted from the soles and by way of welcoming Philip's inspection, he wiggled his toes.

'A warm day, Mr Abrams,' Bella called.

'What of it?' he grumbled.

'A book, in its way,' Bella explained as they walked away.

It was Philip's turn to laugh. 'I had no idea inspiration was so easily come by.'

'What it is, I have asked Miss Skillane to lunch, and I have the most horrible feeling we shall learn more than we actually need to know from her.'

'Then,' Philip teased, 'would it not make more sense to send her packing and ask that old pedlar to lunch? He needs it more and you can winkle his story out of him. Did you not feel, Bella, he had the air of a ruined Russian diplomat with secrets too deep to divulge, with nothing between him and eternity but his wits and a tray of bootlaces?'

'How comical you can be!' she exclaimed. 'How wonderful to sit listening to your chaff in Wiltshire and watching the parson clutch his sides with laughter. How I long for all that. I must be mad to turn it down.'

'Oh dear,' Philip Westland said.

CHAPTER SEVEN

When they returned to Orange Street, they were met with smiles and blushes. Kennett had laid aside his apple and was now holding Mary Skillane's hand. Mrs Venn's eyebrows, as she busied herself laying the table, were signalling a fleet message: Love is in the air! Catching the mood, Philip uncorked and decanted the very best claret to be found in the house.

'For the beef, to be sure,' Mrs Venn cried giddily. 'Which though I say it myself—' But then remembered her place and fled from the room.

'Mary has been telling me about Cornwall,' Kennett murmured. 'It makes me long to go. Did you know the origin of the phrase "hue and cry"? A man—he must be a very gifted man—stands up on the headland and sees the movement of the pilchards under the sea by certain signs and indications. Then he calls out the boats. We could do that, Westland.'

'I'm not sure I would recognise a pilchard if one were on my plate. To know how to find them under the sea—'

'No, no. We shall be the fishermen, braving all weathers, laughing in the teeth of adversity. Mary could wait for us onshore, waving a white handkerchief.'

'Shall we eat?' Bella suggested.

They learned more of Sir William Skillane. Mary's father was from Gwythian, where he had been born in a farm labourer's hovel. At ten he had run away to Falmouth on the other coast. When he was twelve he was listed as captain's servant on board the 32-gunned frigate *Actaeus*. Dismasted by a typhoon in the South China Seas at seventeen, he left the service and took a position with the trading firm of Jameson and Wheatcroft, Penang. He bought his first vessel, a native junk, when he was not yet twenty-two.

'Thus,' Westland suggested, 'a driven man.'

'My father's kind are scattered all over the South China Seas. It is something he always emphasises to strangers. No, what made him was a handful of pearls. He came home, raised money on a Norwegian barque—' she blushed—'this cannot be of the slightest interest—'

'The pearls are the story, Mary,' Kennett interrupted gently.

'Yes, the pearls,' she whispered. 'Of course.'

Kennett stood up from the table and began pacing, his fork still held in his hand. When he found he had it, he threw it absent-mindedly into the fire and there was an unseemly scramble as the whole company leaped to save it. Bella and Philip exchanged glances.

'There is a man,' Kennett said finally, dragging at his red hair, 'a Mr Robert Judd. The son of Beeston Judd, one-time partner to Jameson and Wheatcroft. The father is a notorious rogue and if anything Mr Robert Judd is a bigger scoundrel still. Mary spoke just now of a handful of pearls. There are twenty-seven of them, each as big as my thumbnail. The family legend is that Skillane

69

himself gathered these pearls from a single lagoon and that they result from some especial freak of nature seen nowhere else in the Pacific. Their value is to be measured in the thousands. By now perhaps in five figures.'

'They still exist?' Bella asked. 'They were not used to buy the Norwegian barque that Mary just now mentioned?'

'They comprised the collateral for much of my father's early business affairs,' the girl explained. 'But were never sold. In recent years he has had no need of them.'

'No,' Kennett agreed with heavy emphasis. 'No, indeed. They rest in a Cornish bank vault, inside a red lacquer box. Mary has seen them once only in her life.'

'And Judd?' Westland asked. 'Where does he come into all this?'

Kennett looked towards Mary, who nodded, her fingers kneading the edge of the tablecloth so vigorously that her plate began to move dangerously in the direction of her lap.

'These monster pearls may well have come from some remote lagoon but they were not gathered there by William Skillane. I have Mary's permission to tell you this: her father stole them from a Chinaman in Semarang.'

'I'm not sure—swindled them, perhaps—' she whispered.

'Stole them, swindled them and fled with them back to England. Judd found all this out only two years ago and at once returned to blackmail him.'

'But isn't Sir William now rich enough to pay him off?' Bella asked.

At this point, Mary burst into tears and fled the

room.

'The price he has demanded is Mary's hand in marriage,' Kennett said. 'And thus, in time, a small fortune.'

'And the pearls?'

'Stay right where they are. In the Trevoase Bank. I must go and look for Mary.'

'Philip shall go in your place. You'll oblige me by sitting still, William, and when the summer pudding comes in, eating your portion like a Christian.'

Westland ambled off. On an impulse, Bella reached across the table and kissed the distraught inventor lightly on his forehead.

'I love her!' he declared. 'But even if I didn't, I should count it my duty to set this thing right. I don't know whether Philip told you, but this Judd, this villain, has had the impudence to put up for our club. I saw him yesterday morning—a great beast of a man with the manners of the gutter. He had in tow another slavering idiot, a henchman of some sort. I mean, the very worst kind of thug—'

'Yes,' Bella said, heading him off, 'we can come to that. But tell me first about Sir William. His wealth, his interests.'

'He has eight grain ships in and about the Eastern Mediterranean. All registered to Penzance but considering their home port Tbilisi in the Black Sea, where Skillane has warehouses and godowns. Only four of the captains are British. Three are Russian and there is an American. It is a well-founded and highly profitable company.'

'And in his day Sir William was himself a blue-water sailor, as I think is the expression?'

'He built the whole enterprise up from nothing,

71

using only a complaisant Cornish bank and—I have to admit it—ferocious will-power. He has made a great many Cornishmen rich by their investments and down there he is considered a saint.'

'Poor William,' Bella smiled. 'You have set yourself quite a challenge.'

Just then, Philip Westland led in a red-eyed Mary Skillane. At once her champion jumped up, scattering further cutlery to the carpet, and embraced her. Against all the social proprieties usual for a Sunday lunch, they kissed. Nor was it such a kiss as is bestowed by a gallant uncle upon a swooning niece: Mary gave herself completely to Kennett and he to her. They clung to each other like honeysuckle and vine. Kennett's stance was particularly noteworthy: his eyes closed, an astonished half-smile on his lips, his hands joined in a clasp around her narrow waist.

Smiling herself (and perhaps just a little bit envious, for this was without a doubt first love for both of them), Bella experienced an additional tiny jolt. How it came about she could not say, but the beginning of another Henry Ellis Margam novel had, as it were, tiptoed into the room and laid its hand upon her shoulder. Sir William Skillane was the very figure of a Margam villain, right down to his surname. A coarse and ambitious man is laid low at the moment of his triumph, his nemesis a mysterious figure from the other side of the world. And, trapped in the middle, a girl quite unconscious of her delicate ivory beauty, the blushing champion of the world. The story practically wrote itself.

Bella's publisher, Elias Frean, was in London on a rare foray, staying at a suitably cheap hotel in Gower Street and taking his meals at a restaurant across the Tottenham Court Road.

'A good wine list,' he explained doubtfully. 'It was in this very place that the company was founded. Dear old Naismith, God rest his soul, thought the world of it. The menu has hardly changed in thirty years.'

Nor has the table linen, Bella reflected gloomily. She asked the usual polite questions about Mr Frean's life in France, or at any rate Boulogne. On the face of it the news was not good. His last young man had decamped to Sicily, taking with him a portmanteau of silver and whatever loose change he could find hidden about the place by the notoriously stingy Frean.

'But all that is so much water under the bridge. Indeed, I snap my fingers at it. I am here to engage a manservant of altogether a different cloth. Sergeant Griffiths. Of the 7th Hussars,' he added with a sly smirk.

'You astonish me,' Bella said gallantly.

'An unpolished diamond. Slow in the head, you understand, but a grand figure of a man.'

'And is he presently on duty with the Hussars?'

Frean laughed. 'Bless me, no. We met in Boulogne when he was somewhat on his uppers after twenty years' service to Queen and country. I gave him the fare home and he got work in Wilton, on the Earl of Pembroke's estate. His sister is in service there. She wrote to say that Arthur—that is his name, Arthur—had many fond memories of a

73

certain English gentleman he had come across in la belle France and hoped to see him again one of these days.'

'That is a very romantic yarn,' Bella said admiringly.

The sixty-year-old Frean simpered coyly for a moment or two. 'High compliment indeed from such a weaver of dreams. But I suppose we must come to business. I hope to learn you have another book in prospect for me, Mrs Wallis.'

'It may be so. Have you ever heard of someone called Sir William Skillane?'

She was astonished to see Frean peer into his pudding with a face like thunder.

'I very much hope it was not you who recommended him to the firm. A poor joke if it was.'

Bella was perplexed. 'I am at a loss. You must explain yourself, Mr Frean.'

'His musings—that is the very word he used— his musings were sent to the office here with a request they be published. The world will find this hard to believe, but the manuscript was entitled 'From Cornish Hovel to Cadogan Square, A Sailor's Odyssey'. In a long life, I have grown well accustomed to the vanity of authors, but this fellow takes the biscuit.'

'It is a poor work?'

'Unreadable. Utterly unreadable. It is worse than Mr Motion's *Daphne, Queen of the Clouds*, a book I always hold up to fledgling talents as the worst book ever written.'

'You have corresponded with Sir William, I don't doubt?'

'I returned his manuscript and got back an

74

invitation to Cadogan Square and a chance to meet a person called Judd, apparently as fine a villain as ever sailed the South China Seas.'

'Robert Judd?'

'Oh, don't say you have met these dreadful people!'

'Mr Judd and his companion, a Mr Lintott Edwards, have put up for a club of which friends of mine are members.'

'Lintott Edwards! Yes, that too is a name I recall from Skillane's importunate musings. They must be stopped! Your friends should act.'

Frean hesitated, his tongue flickering. Though they were the only people at table and the man who had served them was peaceably reading a paper by the door to the kitchens, he leaned as far forward as he was able and lowered his voice. 'I will tell you this in the greatest confidence. Skillane may have been all he says he was in the days of his pomp but I have heard rumours of some very ugly business dealings since.'

'To do with pearls, perhaps?'

'Pearls?' he asked confused. 'Are there pearls in the story? No, no, to do with property. I hear he is become one of the biggest slum landlords in London.'

Bella drank the last of her very indifferent wine, careful not to let Frean see the expression in her eyes. To stop the trembling in her hand, she laid it on the tablecloth. She was for a moment back in the cesspit that was Morton's Yard. 'Do you happen to know whereabouts he has invested in property?'

'No, and I shouldn't think he does either. That is all in the hands of this fellow Judd, whom he describes in his book as an inspirational companion. Sir William is far too grand a figure for petty detail. He is, by his own lights, a gentleman. A knight, after all. Though how he came by a title is surely a comment on this ghastly age and nothing at all to do with actual worth.'

'Can you say what was so particularly bad about the work he offered you?'

Frean shrugged. 'In many parts it was a list of ships he commanded, or caused to be built. The rest was shameless name-dropping. Brookes of Sarawak I can suffer but who in Christendom is William Featherstone of Surabaya? Or Chien Lu Tze and his half-dozen brothers? I lost the thread very early on. It is in the end a tale about money. Nobody prates about money, not even in the times we live in.'

'It is said he has built himself a castle in Cornwall.'

'Bah,' Frean retorted. 'I have seen the photograph. The house he has there resembles nothing so much as a county asylum.'

'I am interested in Sir William,' Bella confessed. 'He—or someone very like him—might make a story. But I don't think one can castigate a man merely for being vulgar. I am going to ask your indulgence, Mr Frean. Let me find out more before I commit myself.'

'All I ask, dear lady, is that you don't bring the sea and the Far East into things. Nothing written along those lines will ever succeed in English fiction, you may have my word on it.'

* * *

Bella liked walking and set off down Charlotte Street to recover her spirits. The better sort of passer-by raised his hat to a clear-complexioned and confident woman in her very early forties, elegantly dressed in a steel grey jacket with immense buttons and a matching skirt that she kicked out ahead of her with exceptionally beautiful kid boots.

Her destination was Urmiston and Hannah Bardsoe's house in Shelton Street. She arrived there with an armful of flowers, bought from a barrow in Cambridge Circus. Exercise had helped her digest Frean's ghastly lunch and she banged through the door of Hannah's little shop in fine style, making the bell jump on its bracket.

Sitting in the parlour with his boots off was Captain Quigley. He lay back in his chair with one arm thrown across his brow, tended to by a sardonic Mrs Bardsoe.

'Which he is back from his sleuthing and has had his eye blacked on the train from Gravesend, in an argument with a matelot about sail and steam,' Hannah said with great contentment.

'The argument was about face-whiskers. The naval cove was bearded like the pard, a comment I struck into a general discussion of the present-day navy. He had remarks of his own to make about fish-smelling former soldiers, et cetera, and fisticuffs followed.'

'He was caught a right wallop,' Hannah concluded. 'But enough of that. You shall sit down, Mrs Wallis, and take a pot of tea and a nice bit of ginger cake. Charles is out the back, whittling.'

Bella patted Quigley on the head and walked through the scullery into the tiny and sunless yard.

Urmiston was sanding down a very lifelike representation of a hedgehog, fashioned from redwood and exact in every detail.

'For the shop window,' he explained shyly. 'My crouching hare has been much admired. I daresay you noticed it on your way in.'

'I believe I did,' Bella lied briskly. 'A fine piece of work. How long has Quigley been home?'

'He came straight from the station. I would say, restored to his former impossible self.'

'What it is, Charles, I need your help in a certain matter.'

Over tea and cake, she outlined to the others what little she knew of Sir William Skillane and his connections to slum properties.

'And he lives in Cornwall, the animal?' the Captain cried indignantly.

'And Cadogan Square.'

Quigley peered at her with what he hoped was affection but, what with the black eye, came across as something rather more sinister.

'I bow to your knowledge of the human heart but how on earth you can claim to be a Londoner gripes my guts something awful. Cadogan Square is nothing to write home about, nothing at all. It's not much more than a building site at present, dear lady. I doubt more than three houses have been built.'

'I imagined it somewhat different.'

'It might come nearer to your idea of a London square one of these days but, like I say, at present it's nothing much. You was perhaps thinking of Cadogan Place, though that's no better than it should be, neither. Pont Street's a reasonable address. But Cadogan Square is just so much earthworks.'

'I have been gulled,' Bella said, vexed. 'He made it sound like the best address in Chelsea.'

'Perhaps,' Urmiston suggested quietly, 'it gives a clue to his character. He might be one of those men who confuse the new with the valuable. Or he might be boosting the place for some perceived future advantage.'

'Or,' Mrs Bardsoe suggested, 'he might be just what he sounds like, some ignorant clodhopping peasant. All I know about Cornwall is dressed crabs and that horrible clotted cream they go on about.'

'What he is don't matter,' Quigley grunted, 'except in one respect. Does he have title to that place where Molly breathed her last?'

'That is the question,' Bella agreed.

'It is a point easily settled by half a morning's enquiry,' Urmiston observed uneasily. 'But I invite you to consider, Captain, that even if Sir William is found to own Morton's Yard, that doesn't make him a criminal. It might make him contemptible, but so are a great many men walking about London this evening.'

The swelling around Quigley's eye greatly altered his general expression of facetious good humour, but what he said next shocked them all, his face lending its ugliness to the retort. 'And I invite you to keep your long nose out of it,' he said in a thickened voice.

There was a shocked silence, ended by Mrs Bardsoe taking the Captain by his ear and dragging him out into the scullery. The door slammed behind them and immediately afterwards came the sound of a stinging slap.

'The moment he finds Billy Murch he will tell him of this,' Urmiston whispered. 'And then I wouldn't give a brass farthing for Skillane's life. We can't have it, Bella. You don't kill someone for being a grasping and heartless swine.'

If he was looking for a reply, he waited in vain. Bella refused his glance; and after a moment or two picked up her gloves and hat. She seemed about to say something—even walking down Shelton Street a few moments later she had the distracted air of a woman who regretted not speaking her piece. But finally she trudged on, her chin in her chest. Was Billy Murch—if ever the Captain found him—going to push his way into this story? If he was, then Urmiston was right: Sir William Skillane's life was not worth a brass farthing.

CHAPTER EIGHT

Sir William Skillane is in his carriage, on the way to a charity lunch in the City. Today is the first outing for an astounding morning dress of the palest pink cloth, a colour his tailor has described (not without anguish) as pearl blush. This tint, when seen next to men wearing a more conservative grey, or black, seems outrageous: but nothing in Sir William's wealth is to be understated. Money speaks. When it is asked in the clubs who made the largest donation at this lunch, it will be answered by some 'the man in the pink suit'.

By long habit, he rises at six. He makes his own coffee and enjoys what he thinks of as the continental breakfast. It was taught him long ago by a Dutch trader and accordingly Sir William is the only man in London to start the day with a slice of ham, a boiled egg and wafer-thin cheese. At eight he bathes and shaves.

Sir William goes direct from his bathroom to his desk. He has a balding blond—another Dutchman—he describes to others as a personal secretary. Wouters is discretion personified: he has the manners of an executioner and a completely fearless attitude towards money.

'Because it is not yours we play with, but mine,' Skillane has suggested more than once.

'Because it is only money,' Wouters invariably replies.

His wife would like him to steal from his employer, or at the very least search for advantage in his unusual position. But Wouters was in his day a professional gambler. He knows money is only a tide, a ceaseless ebb and flow of something essentially meaningless and unremarkable.

In 1871, at the height of the Paris Siege, Wouters was in Monte Carlo. He played the tables for eleven hours without missing a turn of the wheel and came away with as many francs as there are sparrows in London. In the hotel that night, three men broke into his room and beat him senseless. When he came round, the money had gone, save for a few hundred francs thrown carelessly on to the bed. Wouters shrugged and after a pause for breakfast, consulted the rail timetable.

Sir William never gambles and likes to know in detail where his money is working. However, he has a precept: only what is new need be discussed at these daily meetings. There is no map in his study, no works of reference. Wouters reads cables to him, some commercial, some of a political nature. No minutes are kept. Skillane prides himself on a prodigious memory and (if he were honest) a swindler's caution with the written word.

'You say Simeonovski is at anchor in Syracuse these last five days,' he interrupts Wouters suddenly. 'Why is that?'

'His wife is dying of cholera.'

Skillane inspects his secretary with pale blue eyes. 'You are sure of that?'

'The lady is not yet twenty years of age. They are devoted to each other.'

Skillane considers briefly, waves his hand for Wouters to continue. A bridge across the Mandru in the Bulgarian province of Burgas has collapsed, delaying a consignment of tobacco to the port. On the other side of the Black Sea, another of Sir William's vessels has clashed with brigands.

'Whereabouts?'

Wouters glances down at his notes. 'Ochyemchiri.'

'The dogs in the streets have more character than the Governor of that province. Pay him. Anything else?'

Wouters inclines his head to indicate that he has come to the end of his report. Sir William lumbers to his feet and leaves the room without a word.

And here he is at last in his newish carriage, rattling along Sloane Street, plucking his nostril, worrying a little about his health. There was a time when he could take a turn and turn about with the bow oar, rowing his ship through a dead calm, but those days are behind him. His gut hangs, his chest is white and plump. Even walking upstairs to bed is a burden.

His eye is suddenly caught by something untoward. Running alongside the carriage, sometimes in the roadway, sometimes on the pavement, is a gaunt, spare-looking man with an absolutely empty expression. In Knightsbridge the carriage stops for traffic: the man turns and faces directly into the window. To Sir William's amazement, he takes one step, two, until the men are as close as gentlemen in club armchairs, separated only by glass. When the coachman Joplin tickles up the paired horses, the man on the pavement steps back. Sir William relaxes. Though he has learned it is bad form to smoke inside a carriage, even one's own, he lights a cigar.

In Piccadilly, the man reappears, running without effort. Joplin has had enough and, leaning over from his seat, flicks his whip at the scoundrel. The man catches its tip, wraps it around his fist and there is a lurch as he mounts the box for a second or so. Something is said, Skillane cannot hear what.

'I wouldn't try that again if I were you, matey,' the man has commented in a horribly neutral way. He jumps off the box steps and resumes running.

All the way up the Charing Cross Road, all the way along Holborn, the runner keeps pace with the carriage. Skillane has tried to shrink back against the horsehair cushions. Even by the haphazard standards of sanity to be found on London streets among the poor, this is no ordinary fellow.

Sir William has with him a cane with an embossed silver top. Very well. As soon as his carriage reaches his destination he will jump out and roundhouse the madman, lash him across the face. If he goes down, he will kick him. Whether this is the action of a gentleman or not, Sir William does not care. He will not be outfaced by a beggarman. Sumatra rules will apply. The carriage slows, he braces himself for a leap down to the pavement. Within the space of ten seconds or so, however, the man has disappeared.

Skillane looks around him, annoyed at how foolish he must seem to the men and women greeting each other outside the restaurant before going into lunch. One of the most quizzical examinations he receives is from a blonde woman with grey eyes, dressed in what he judges to be a very fashionable costume of brown velveteen. She shows every appearance of recognising him. But, red in the cheeks and mightily flustered, he cannot for the moment place her. After a moment, she turns away. He follows into the restaurant, the glamour of his pearl-pink morning dress somewhat diminished. He is still carrying his elegant cane halfway along the shaft, like a savage.

*　　　*　　　*

Bartholdy's was handsomely decorated with flowers presented by the Gardeners' Company, for the lunch was given by the philanthropist Walter Curtice, who was a liveried member. Bella could have done with fewer blooms: the long room in which they ate had a clerestory roof and the overall effect was that of a gathering held in a greenhouse. About sixty guests sat down to the plainest of plain fare, saved by some excellent wines. The purpose of the lunch was charitable, for the amiably earnest

84

Mr Curtice wished to bring forward a scheme to create what he called sailors' lending libraries, depots of improving literature that would eventually encircle the world, bringing solace to lonely men in foreign ports. Sir William Skillane had put up a thousand pounds and was the guest of honour. Bella was seated next to a former Surgeon of the Fleet, an incredibly old and wrinkled man, who wanted to talk chiefly about petit point, a hobby he had taken up to please his wife, that had in time become an obsession. On her right hand was a sprawling and sardonic Robert Judd.

'I have found that sailors are perfectly capable of finding their own solace in foreign ports,' he said, with a curiously animal frankness. 'I will not name the means. Are you a do-gooder, Mrs Wallis? Are you one who would Christianise the heathen, for example?'

'Why, Mr Judd,' she replied calmly, 'I have not the time to help you, I'm afraid. But if you are anxious about the matter, I can certainly point you in the direction of those who can. Across the table is Bishop Duddington, for example. He might take up your case.'

Judd hesitated quite a long time before laughing—or, perhaps a better description would be, barking like a seal. 'In my case salvation must wait.'

'I have always understood that to be the guiding principle of most business,' Bella agreed.

She was interested in him. Though Judd's clothes had clearly been tailored and were of the very latest cut, he wore them uneasily, as if having been forced into travesty. (Witness the cuff to his sleeve, bearing the marks of the butter dish.) No

85

matter how hard he tried to disguise it, there was a kind of truculence about him that undid all his superficial polish. He was a boor.

'Where might one find you in London, Mrs Wallis?' he asked.

'What a very impertinent question, Mr Judd.'

'Is it? I am grown weary of London manners.'

'Things are ordered differently in the East, is that it?'

'Then you know who I am?'

'Your sentiments about good manners have preceded you. What is it like in Penang? What do you have there? Pearls? Coconuts?'

He studied her with pale green eyes, like a cat. 'What made you say pearls?'

Only then did she realise what she had said. 'Coconuts, then.'

'But you said pearls.'

'It's what one imagines,' Bella said. 'Rubies. Jade. Pirates.'

'Pirates,' Judd scoffed, still with his gaze on her.

'I have heard of pirates in that region, I fancy.'

'There are giants there. Or perhaps you need a giant's strength to make your way.'

'Say in the manner of your patron, Sir William?'

'Sir William,' he said in a neutral tone, 'is a great man. And as you have seen today, a very great philanthropist.'

'From Cornwall, I understand.'

'Yes, from Cornwall. Have you been there?'

'Not yet. Is it a man's world down there, too?' She had begun to resent his catlike attention. 'I will tell you what it is, Mr Judd: you are trying too hard. I know you to be very wealthy. It's true I know nothing of Penang or Cornwall. I know a little about men, however, and you are too full of your own conceit to be interesting.' She smiled.

Judd ducked his head as if in defeat but his neck was red with anger. 'You have a waspish tongue, madam.'

'I see the lunch is breaking up. Before she goes, I will introduce you to Lady Tenterden. I know for a fact she adores Cornwall. Her husband was a sea-officer for many years in Eastern waters.'

Sir John Tenterden was an Admiral of the Blue in his day. Buried in Trincomalee in '67, he was exhumed by his widow and reburied in the family vault at Staveley. As for a love of Cornwall, only a wit would ascribe that to Kitty, whose sole connnection to the duchy was falling into the sea at Falmouth, blown there by spring gales after an over-exuberant dinner aboard her husband's first command, the *Minerva*.

'Good God, Bella,' she exclaimed in the cab that took them back towards the West End. 'You do know thc most incredible people. That fellow Judd has thighs on him like a carthorse. I worry for him. His trouser arrangements might burst at any moment.'

'Did you talk to him about Penang?'

'He asked me if I knew William Kennett.'

'How should you?' Bella asked, alarmed.

'Kennett is our neighbour in Chiswick. What this fellow wanted with the information I can't imagine. But about those thighs. Did you notice them?'

'I can't say that I did.'

Kitty Tenterden, like Bella a widow, was well into her seventies. She took Bella's hand, bouncing it on her bony knee. 'No gentleman has such legs.

But let's ask the cab to drive us around a while. I want to know how things progress with that delightful man Westland. You can be quite frank with me, Bella dearest. Everybody knows I am the soul of discretion.'

They directed the cabman to drive to Park Lane and sat for a while looking out on to the Park. Lady Tenterden bored very quickly of Philip Westland's virtues and began a long account of the latest gossip from Marlborough House. A lady compromised by the Prince of Wales had been taken by her husband to Mentone to repent of her ways. There she had eloped with an Austrian colonel of artillery, who spirited her away to his estate in Carinthia.

'Wherever that might be,' Kitty concluded sniffily. 'But altogether a very unfashionable address, I should imagine.'

Bella laughed gently but was taken aback by her friend's next remark, delivered in the same mannered and floaty way.

'Marry him, Bella,' Kitty Tenterden said. 'Westland, I mean. Someone told me the other day you won't marry him because you love him too much. What piffle you young girls do talk from time to time. It has to do with novels, I am sure.'

*   *   *

On his own initiative, Captain Quigley went undercover at Cadogan Square. But not quite undercover. He sat comfortably on a pile of sand, looking directly into the windows of the Skillane house, smoking a stub of pipe and scratching his thigh from time to time. It was a mild afternoon,

88

with watery sunshine, and the trenches and scaffolds of the builders' site were empty. Quigley could hear a skylark.

'Every inch the British workman,' Jacko Watson cried, joining him with a bacon sandwich he obligingly halved.

'And I have my shovel to hand,' the Captain protested mildly. 'I don't see too many of your mates running amok with the hods and wheelbarrows.'

'Down the boozer,' Jacko explained. 'Waiting on the ganger to come back from looking for the clerk of works. Houses like these, you don't just run 'em up, Perce. Every detail has to be just so. All the plaster work's done by a set of jabbering Eyeties. At I don't know what cost a running foot. As for the bathrooms, the Queen could have her dinner off the floor in there.'

'If she was so minded,' Quigley said absently.

'Correct.'

'I was meaning to ask you, Jacko: have you heard tell of Billy Murch at all recently?'

'I get it,' Jacko Watson said. 'I was wondering what you was doing sniffing about down here. Lost your pal, have you?'

'You haven't seen him, then?'

'That middle house, the one you are eyeing so assiduous? Belongs to a cove called Sir Edward or Sir William Skillane. The usual bag of lard. Daughter a nice bit, though. Yes, Billy called by first thing this morning.'

'You don't say so?' Quigley yelped. 'This very morning?'

'Drunk as a skunk and the hour not gone seven by this here watch of mine. He had some business

89

with his lordship, seemingly. But I told him, you don't want to mess with Skillane. Oh no.'

'So what did he say to that? Did he mention the nature of his business with the Cornish gent?'

'I think he'd like to blow him up. At the very least.'

'Could be,' the Captain mused uneasily.

'Blow him up while he's sat on the throne in one of his three bleeding bathrooms. Just raising one cheek to ease hisself, paper open at the racing tissue—'

'I have the picture, Jacko.'

'You haven't seen old Billy yourself, then?'

'Would I be asking all these questions if I had, like?'

'Well, don't get shirty. Where're you off now?'

'I have to report this to the Home Secretary. Who's waiting on my word.'

'Bollocks,' Jacko said comfortably.

*　　　*　　　*

'You expected to find Quigley here,' Bella suggested to the figure hunched in the Fleur de Lys office. He had the fighting man's caution with enclosed spaces and sat with his chair dragged around to the open door, his feet drawn up under his knees, boots flat to the floorboards. He was in silhouette and sat quite still. The only thing that moved was the smoke from his cheroot. It drifted for a brief moment and then was snatched by the tiny tornado that never left the deep well of brick they sat in.

'I came to see you,' he muttered. 'You sense that I'm in drink and you'd be right. I haven't been

90

rightly sober since—since that night in Holborn.'

'Have you eaten today?' Bella asked in what she hoped was a neutral tone, as an another might enquire whether it was raining outside.

Billy Murch shook his head. 'Not important.'

'Billy, look at me. Turn your head and look at me.'

He did as she asked. Scabs of dried blood were caught in his growth of beard and his eyes were red-rimmed and tortured.

'I know you have been to lunch today with that villain Skillane—I ran alongside his carriage for a couple of miles or more, just so's he could get a proper gander at me. I was for dragging him out in front of his rich friends and killing him with my bare hands, you understand. And then I saw you.'

She waited. But he had exhausted what explanation he was going to make. He looked at his cheroot and threw it away. It bounced on the pavement of the courtyard, making a shower of tiny red sparks. Bella watched as he knuckled his eye-sockets with filthy hands.

'This man Skillane—not a man, this slug—owns the house that Molly died in. That rathole and a hundred others like it. He is a slum landlord to beat all.'

'How did you find this out?'

'By asking. By wading chest-high through his filth. D'you remember the lodging-house keeper at Randall's? He was my start. And don't he wish he'd never been born. You hear it said about people, they are maddened by grief. But not me, I thought, never me.'

'You say you saw me today and that altered things.'

91

Murch shrugged. 'She died in his house. Starved to death in Skillane's house and still paid him tuppence a day for the privilege. I want revenge, is what I want. Or justice. You and Mr Urmiston take the long view about this sort of thing, I know that. I've never met Mr Westland, nor his mate neither, though I would welcome the chance. I need help. That is the long and short of it. Thought I could handle myself. Find I can't.'

The chair he was sitting in was a recent acquisition of the Captain's, an applewood Windsor with handsome curved arms supported by pilasters. Murch's right hand tightened and the chair-arm on that side of his body snapped off with a crack like a rifle. Bella rose and took the debris from Billy before drawing him to her. His head lolled against her chest and he sobbed like a child.

'You will come home with me. Mr Westland is the one to talk to, you are right. But first you will eat some soup and a plate of ham and pickles. Here's money. I put you upon your word to turn up at Orange Street within the hour. Do you understand me?'

'I'm in no state to be—'

She took a step back and held his chin in both hands. 'Within the hour,' she repeated.

*　　　*　　　*

Bella's instinct was right—Philip Westland was just the person to talk to Murch. After the merest of introductions, Philip waved Bella away out of the room. The two men sat with their feet in the grate in the downstairs sitting room, each with a brandy to hand and a cigar.

'I have been experimenting recently with a pipe,' Westland said. 'A friend invented something along the lines of a portable hookah—anyway, there's water involved. Draws well but makes a noise like pulling a boot from the mud. Did you ever—?'

'In the Crimea, yes.'

'Weren't you very young?'

'What it is, Mr Westland, sir, today I came as close to killing a man in broad daylight as can be imagined. A fat old man I did not know existed a fortnight ago. I ran alongside his carriage—'

'Yes, Bella told me about that.'

Murch studied him carefully. 'The actions of a madman, do you think?'

'Mr Murch, the one thing I do not think about you is that you're mad.'

They sat on for a few moments, listening to the heavy tick of a case clock. Westland had the great gift of patience. Though the two had met for the first time only twenty minutes or so ago, he had formed a view of the man opposite that he knew he would never change. He was responding to the honesty in Billy Murch, his elaborated seriousness.

'I have a friend,' he heard himself saying, '—the same friend who is the inventor of the portable water pipe—who also wants justice. And from the same family. Mrs Wallis has told me how resourceful you are. I propose we put you and Mr Kennett—that is my friend's name—together in some way. How, exactly, I don't know—but I think you should meet.'

'Does the gentleman live in London?'

'On the Surrey side of the river.'

'I am no man's servant,' Murch warned.

'You know about Mrs Wallis that she is also

93

Henry Ellis Margam? You know she finds her plots in the immediate here and now? Your friend Skillane and another man called Robert Judd are in her mind—if you like, under her gaze. It is my job to care for Bella. And yours to look out for William Kennett—the man who invented the portable water pipe. Skillane and his partners look like black mischief to me, Billy.'

'She is writing about them?'

'I believe she is.'

'Then I am of your party,' Billy Murch said simply. The two men rose to shake hands.

'Nothing brutal now,' Westland could not help himself adding.

Billy Murch's smile was thin indeed. 'As to that, we must see,' he muttered. 'If you will give me a note, I will walk across to Chiswick now. And introduce myself.'

'Yes,' Westland said uncertainly. 'That would be the ticket.'

CHAPTER NINE

It was agreed by many a London hostess that there was nothing more bankable than an invitation to Mrs Bella Wallis at least once in the season. She was calm, pleasantly undemonstrative and adept at light and inconsequential conversation. Old men delighted in her company and women who had something to lose—like a gloomy husband or an over-romantic son—could find no danger in her. Quite the contrary—she was as chaste as Arctic snow. If she had a fault at all, it was that from time to time—as now—she simply disappeared.

'I know her very well,' Cissie Cornford explained. 'And I'm sure she would count me as her dearest confidante. This is nothing new. For three months of the year, she is not at home to anyone.'

'Some say she is very poor,' Mrs Titmarch suggested.

'Oh, as to that, who is poor these days? We are all comfortably placed. I know Titmarch is a mere rural dean but they look after such people quite well in Somerset, I believe. No, it is not money. I would never tell this to another living soul, you understand, but—' She touched a bony forefinger to her temple and tapped twice.

Mrs Titmarch was astounded. 'Can nothing be done?' she cried.

'Tragically, not,' Lady Cornford said with the greatest complacency, repositioning her false teeth with a gentle sucking sound. 'A little more of the almond cake, Mrs Titmarch?'

'But such an amiable figure of a woman! Is it the loss of her dear husband that causes the grief, do you think?'

'Oh dear,' Cissie sighed airily. 'I fear I have said too much.'

Like almost anything else she asserted for a fact, by nightfall she had forgotten she had said it.

The truth was much simpler. Bella was now in daily occupancy of Fleur de Lys Court; or better to say it was Henry Ellis Margam at the rosewood table, sending out for lunch, smoking a little too much, shouting for silence when the three clerks in the next-door office larked about or strangers came into the Court to settle differences that had arisen out on the main pavement. Each day, from mid-morning to four in the afternoon, the pages piled up slowly at Bella's elbow, a story that was hers yet not hers. Margam drank Niersteiner, Bella went home with the headache.

Captain Quigley was used to these early stages of composition—or fits of scribbling, as he put it. He moved a chair into the yard, where he sat with one leg cocked on the knee of the other, doing sentry duty. From time to time Bella heard him in low-voiced conversation with one or other of his circle of friends: it was an unbothering noise, like bees in a summer pasture. Sometimes he would pull out a turnip watch, glance at the time and slope off to the Coal Hole or the Cyder Cellars for a little refreshment. There he would harbour dark thoughts about Sir William Skillane.

'If a certain knight of the realm was to walk through them doors,' he would observe to acquaintances like Welsh Phil, 'I would up and chin him, so help me. Not a word spoke, not so much as a how d'ye do, but boosh!'

'And how comes it like that, Perce?'

'There are dark deeds afoot, my old cocker.'

'There always is down your side of the street. This knight of the realm—a chancer, is he?'

'A right bastard.'

'Just asking for a visit from Uncle Slap, would you say?' asked Welsh Phil hopefully, who was the originator of that useful term.

'You put it very neat.'

But what grieved the Captain more than Skillane's skulduggery—though he sensed in some obscure way the two were connected—were the mysterious goings-on of his old pal Billy Murch.

Quigley had walked over to Kennington, where he had been told Billy had a room in Stannary Place, next to the park: but his bird had flown. Or perhaps—most bitter thought of all—had never been there in the first place. The door was opened by a Russian beanpole with a beard down to his waistcoat, who signed in dumb-show that he spoke no English and (an eloquent shrug) had never heard of Billy Murch.

'How did you know he was Russian?' Bella asked.

'No snow on his boots but a very low sort of place for all that,' the Captain explained. 'Nothing but cabbage on the hob, children everywhere. A goat roaming about the front room.'

'Doesn't that strengthen the view that Billy did not lodge there?'

'Very like,' Quigley retorted, who had his suspicions that the lady knew more than she was letting on. 'But I know the regard you hold Miss Skillane in. I will just say this. Her esteemed dad could end up on the dining-room table with two pennies in his eyes. A great man for bearing a grudge, Billy.'

*   *   *

The plot that Bella devised for the tale of Sir William was all to do with a ridiculous old fraud and his beautiful daughter. It was a story of London society. Some parts were easier to create than others. The back room in Bartholdy's restaurant had become Skillane's conservatory. As to the famous address, Bella took Quigley at his word and moved the house from Cadogan Square to Holland Park, an area she associated with the more enigmatic rich. Her own dressmaker lived in the squalid end of Pottery Lane (where she was assembling a quiet fortune) and Skillane was now to be found in a fine stucco house at the top end.

Cornwall stubbornly resisted her attempts to describe it. She knew no one other than Urmiston who had been there or wished to visit: if there were to be rocks and wild men in the story, maybe Scotland would do, or further afield, Georgia. She considered she had a score to pay off with Cissie Cornford and that harmless gossip became a gypsy woman with a loose tongue, roaming the moors—if there were moors in Cornwall—in a donkey-cart, cadging tobacco from soldiers.

Mary Skillane was of course the damsel in distress. Bella liked writing about her, more than was strictly proper. Mary in bed, Mary dressing with extreme care in the morning, the better to conceal a gold chain no thicker than a hair given to her by her secret lover one delirious evening at the theatre. Mary at bathtime, Mary swimming illicitly in some rock-strewn cove, her pale limbs scissoring the green waves.

Skillane himself was straight out of Thackeray. Bella had once met a man who wrote to the master when *A Book of Snobs* was being serialised, asking if he, the poor innocent, could be considered a snob. Thackeray put him straight into the next episode, so thinly disguised that even his cook could recognise the original. Sir William was a similar gift to fiction: he passed from real life to caricature with no more fuss than a man changing trains at Reading. Mary's father spent a great deal of time in these early drafts eating mutton and bullying the servants. The piece of plot that pleased Bella most was when she sent him to a bookseller's in Museum Street, where he ordered fifty books on any old subject, providing the bindings were calf.

The Skillane pearls interested her but she was struggling to find a convincing portrait of her hero, using William Kennett as her model. She reinvented him as a soldier, the impecunious Lord Attlesford. Attlesford looked like his original— that beguiling mouth—but shared none of Kennett's reckless scientific enthusiasms. Lord Attlesford, on leave from the Blues, fought for the Turks against the Russians, spied for his country in Afghanistan and was a man possessed of daemonic fits of melancholy. At his house in Shropshire, he spent a great deal of time looking out on to the home paddock, reflecting bitterly on those who had the aristocratic virtues and those who had not.

And there he might have languished, dwindled and died (for Bella was growing bored with a man who spent so much time looking out of the window and was all for starting the novel again with less of Thackeray and a better hero) were it not for the stone thrown into these placid waters by Molucca Edwards, Robert Judd's colleague and myrmidon.

*   *   *

Molucca Edwards was finding London irksome. Skillane had Cadogan Square to amuse him, Bob Judd the simpering Skillane daughter. Molucca had a fat wallet and the company of Mrs Givens, a genial whore he met at Brighton races one dank afternoon. He brought her back to London and

99

they set up together in Elm Park Gardens, off the Fulham Road. Four ground-floor rooms, never fewer than two dozen empty bottles ranged along the sitting room wall, a bed like a hayrick after it had been struck by lightning.

Liza Givens had wide experience of men but never had she taken up with quite such a rough diamond as dear old Molucca. He had money to burn, apparently, but about as much charm as an outside privy. He ate prodigiously, drank himself senseless most nights, and in between retold the course of his life in the China Seas. Most of his yarns involved biffing, as he called it. It seemed there was not a foreign devil he had not knocked senseless, gutted with Susan (the name he gave to his knife) or simply thrown overboard for the sharks.

'I squared up to him,' he was fond of saying, 'and looked him in the eye. I have my own way of doing that.'

'And don't I know it,' Liza Givens agreed feelingly.

'Looked him in the eye, never saying a word. He's holding a musket, remember, and I have nothing but Susan. Now then, I can feel the deck tremble beneath my feet, can sense what more's to come when we leave the lee of the island and the old tub falls off a point or two and I'm ready—'

'Was your pal Mr Judd with you this particular trip?' Liza interrupted.

Molucca stared at her. 'And ain't you always going on about Bob Judd?' he complained in a nasty sort of voice.

'He fascinates me.'

'He wouldn't if you knew him at all. I could tell

100

you stories about Juddy—'

'Well, go on then, tell us one.'

But he was saved the trouble: the man in question arrived shortly after.

What fascinated Liza Givens about Judd was the way he treated Molucca, putting her in mind of a man with the ownership of a devoted but dim-witted dog. Disdaining the use of a chair (as if Molucca had invited him merely to a playful tussle on the carpet), he wiped the mantel with the palm of his hand before laying his elbow on it. And there he posed. His sneer was magnificent. Liza was entranced by his boots, of the finest kid. He was a thug, like Molucca; but a dandy into the bargain.

'I have found where Westland hangs his hat,' he said in his brutal languid way.

Liza immediately offered to excuse herself, for when business was being talked among such men as these, she had always found it wiser to be deaf and blind. Judd waved his hand with the greatest negligence. She was no more real to him than the fire tongs or the armchair in which Molucca sat. (And he, poor chump, looking as confused as a girl.)

'Westland? And who's he when he's at home?' Molucca asked.

Judd sighed, looking at his lieutenant as if at a black beetle, or an earwig. 'You may remember how we put up for membership of a toff's club in Ebury Street?'

'It was no skin off my nose that they wouldn't have us.'

'No, I'm sure it wasn't. This Westland and his chum had us black-balled, however. Which means he put the boot in with the committee. Perhaps we

101

hadn't been to the right schools.'

Despite herself, Liza snorted out a laugh. She was rewarded by a boxed ear, delivered by Molucca with enough force to shake the pins out of her hair.

'There's more to it than that, though?' he asked.

There was: but what was the point of telling an oaf like Molucca? Judd had plans for the future that did not include his henchman and these plans were poised very delicately. The Wallis woman was a dangerous adversary, moreover one surrounded and apparently protected by a rum crew he was finding it hard to fathom.

'Let's say that this gentleman needs a warning-off,' he suggested, putting it in terms that Molucca could grasp. 'He is getting under my feet. So I asked myself, who could I depend upon to put the fear of God up him.'

At last Molucca's frown lifted. He understood. It was the kind of work he knew how to do. On jobs like this, it was an advantage not to delve too deep into Bobby Judd's motives. Dear old Bob had his way of going about things that often involved meetings down dark alleys: the outcome had always proved satisfactory in the past. Pointed in the right direction by the boss, Molucca had once taken a scrawny Australian chancer out to meet the sharks off Suyala Point, after relieving him of three hundred American silver dollars. Lifted him clean off the dock, decorated him with a few slashing wounds and later, after chucking in a few buckets of blood and fishguts, pitched him over the side.

When he reported back, Judd had told him to keep the money with as much nonchalance as another man might dust down his jacket. Good old Bob.

'What do you want done?' he asked Judd now.

'He must have something wicked happen to him.'

Molucca was struck by a bright idea. 'It isn't the other cove we should be talking about? The daddy longlegs from Chiswick, the one your girl is sweet on?'

Judd stared. 'What's that again?'

'No, no,' Molucca said hastily. 'I have it clear now. Do you want me to off him, this Westland?'

'Won't be necessary. Just give that knife of yours a bit of an outing. Give him something hideous to remember us by. Mark his card, if you want to put it that way. Mind, if you kill him, you're on your own.'

'And Sir William? How does he stand with all this?'

Liza flinched. She could have told Molucca: he was asking too many questions. Judd sighed. He swept his forearm along the mantelpiece, knocking everything that stood there to the grate. The landlady's lustre vases shattered, her clock lay on its back, shocked into silence. Judd took a fold of paper from his waistcoat pocket and laid it on the newly cleared black marble surface. He tapped it with his forefinger.

'A useful address. Remember, this is the fat-arse that had you pegged for an ignorant know-nothing son of a whore.'

'He said that? He used those very words?'

'Said you were neither use nor ornament to the human race. That he was surprised to find you could speak or walk upright. That your mother was nothing better than a mattress.'

'The blind impudence,' Molucca growled.

But in truth, he was not all that disappointed about being shown the door by the Waverdon Club; it was exactly the sort of place that made him feel uneasy. On his only visit he had tipped the waiter extravagantly and suffered the indignity of having his loose silver returned to him, less a sixpence. When interviewed by the committee, his remark that a man needed a place to drink from time to time without the company of thirsty women went down badly. His application for membership needed to be sponsored by an existing member. Molucca was on the back foot here, too. He could not remember the name of the man whom he had met at the Café Royal.

'An old gent,' he temporised. 'Mutton chop whiskers, some sort of Indian Army connections. Maybe a bit touched in the head.'

He was describing a past president of the Waverdon, Colonel Sir Ernle Hollis VC, hero of Shivavasrani.

'What it is,' he said to Liza Givens, after Judd had left, 'it don't sit with me too well, all this side of things. Bob Judd loves it. But there's nothing much here in London for me, d'you see?'

'You was born here, wasn't you?'

'At Wapping, yes. I'm talking about all this mincing about with the how d'ye do and doncha know coves. All this "my good fellow, my dear old chum" malarkey. You know me. I'm a plain man.'

Yes, Liza thought gloomily, I'll say that about you. None plainer.

If it had been her job to mark Philip Westland for life, she would have gone about it with some urgency—that same evening would hardly have seemed too soon. She had a whore's realism in this: Molucca might be a violent man but his rages blew out quickly. His friend Judd was all the more frightening for being so icy cold. Molucca was the Catherine wheel, spinning haplessly on its pin. Robert Judd was the rocket. Aimed, she thought wincingly, right up the jacksie.

All these reflections she shared the next day with Daisy Lawrence, an old friend from Newport Street, when the world was younger. Daisy had done well for herself, finding and marrying a German butcher in a small way of business and working him to death. He dropped dead over the brisket one frosty January morning. She still had the shop, run these days by a gormless and adoring lad called Alf.

'This Molucca sounds a right turd,' she observed, her language not matching the elegance of her feathered hat and purple bombazine dress, nor her pale lemon gloves.

They were drinking in St Martin's Lane, at a pub favoured by theatricals. It was very much a venue to suit Daisy, all etched glass and velvet benches, where champagne was served on tap.

'I have got myself in with a rum crowd,' Liza admitted. 'They're a no good lot and that's no lie. Molucca hasn't got the brains he was born with but his mate Judd is a dangerous bugger.'

She outlined the visit Judd had made and the plan to cut some unlucky gent called Westland. Daisy listened largely without comment as to the commission Molucca had been given: the kind of men both these women knew best were prone to sort things out with knives and clubs. But she had a duty of kindness to her friend.

'I should bunk off it if I were you, Liza. It don't sound right. Wasn't you after the cove that had the linen shop in Brighton?'

'That all fell through,' Liza said, tersely.

'Well, I never,' Daisy said in a scolding sort of voice. 'After all the hard work you put in.'

'It was going along fine and then he had his leg off.'

'No woman wants that.'

'There was a tearful parting. I go up the racecourse for something a bit more cheery and before I've finished me first glass, there's old Molucca in front of me. The big ape.'

'Staring at you like you was a choice bunch of bananas.'

'More or less.'

This thread might have been teased out much longer, had not Liza suddenly jumped up with a yelp. 'Blind me if that isn't old Percy Quigley passing outside.'

'The Captain? Ask the old sot to join us. I haven't seen him for ten years or more. Go on, girl, run after him. Let's have his remarks pertinent to the problem.'

*   *   *

Quigley's report was rambling but unequivocal. Bella listened with a dark face. She was very unamused to learn that her address was known to Robert Judd. Nor was she made any happier to hear Philip Westland bluster that he was a match for Mr Edwards or any other thug who came at him with a knife. Quigley had gone on town patrol to Elm Park Gardens and reported that Molucca was quite as big as Liza described and, though he did not exactly trail his knuckles along the pavement, had shoulders on him that would not disgrace an orang-utanio.

'Which is?' she asked frostily.

'One of your bigger apes. A gorilla, if it's easier to picture.'

'The point is,' Westland said emphatically, 'I do not plan to hide under the bed here, waiting for him to turn up.'

Quigley's coughing harrumph was more eloquent than any speech he might have made.

'I shall get Kennett to teach me the rudiments of boxing,' Philip explained.

'And what on earth does he know about such a thing?'

'Very well then, a better idea. The Captain shall furnish me with a swordstick.'

'Can be arranged,' Quigley nodded quickly. 'From the estate of a Belgian gentleman, late of Tavistock Square. But, before you was to unsheath it, might I suggest a handful of ground pepper flung into the eyes first? Nothing assists the old cut and thrust more.'

Bella slapped the arm of her chair with impatience. 'I cannot see what they have to gain by mutilating you. Unless it is a thrust at Kennett, to warn him off canoodling with the Skillane girl. A high price for you to pay.'

'What is annoying you most,' Philip said quietly, 'is the fact that Judd knows where you live. I take it this has never happened before. It suggests to me that you are the real target of his viciousness. In some way we don't yet understand, art has collided

107

with life. Taking them all together as a gang, they sense you know something they do not wish you to divulge.'

'Do you have a notion what that might be?'

'A man comes home from the East with stolen pearls of the highest value. They are the secret collateral in all his business dealings. Some years later he is made a knight of the realm. His whole standing in society is compromised if the story of the pearls comes out. He is prepared to pimp his own daughter to keep the secret safe.'

'My God,' Bella said faintly, suddenly remembering the conversation with Judd at the charity lunch in the City. 'What have I done?'

Westland and Quigley exchanged glances. 'What have you done?' Westland asked.

'When I met Mr Judd, I found him repellent enough to score points off him. I did not notice then that I had said too much.'

'You did not mention the Skillane pearls, for all love?' Westland asked.

'Of course not,' Bella said sharply. 'I am not quite so stupid. But I did say something careless about pearls in general.'

She held out her glass to be filled with a shaking hand. 'I have brought this down on us.'

'What you said gave him the idea that you knew more about the pearls than you revealed?'

'I think so,' Bella said in a very small voice.

'So, what are we going to do about it?' Quigley asked.

She moved to the window and peered out into Orange Street. There were few faces she did not recognise. Though it was not yet quite dark, Mr Gough the greengrocer had lit his naphtha lamps

108

and stood among the boxes in his pavement display, eating an apple and talking to the musician Hubison. Mrs Allen was gossiping with Mrs Shipley. In fact, all the Orange Street neighbours were as carefully disposed as an operatic chorus: part of the pleasure in living in such a short street was that people did more or less the same things at the same time, from servants taking out the mats to be shaken in the early morning to their mistresses drawing down the blinds at night.

'How will he go about this work?' she asked Quigley absent-mindedly.

'Not by day. Stealth and sunlight don't go together. He won't try it in an empty street neither. Mr Westland is a novice at this kind of thing, but you don't need eyes in the back of your head to see the danger in that, not if he's the only other cove about, d'you see?'

Bella glanced at Westland, who nodded.

'I am generally cautious in such circumstances, yes,' he said.

'So, by night, in a crowded street? It doesn't sound too plausible.'

Quigley joined her at the window. 'I don't know about that. Those two fellows squaring up outside the pub, for instance. Are they going for the knives and dusters, or are they just a couple of drunks?'

'One of them is Mr Smallbones, the coalman. The other is his brother-in-law.'

Quigley raised his eyebrows and was about to say more but Westland laid a restraining hand on his sleeve. 'The Captain's point is that every pavement around here has such night-time scenes. It's not in the least unusual. It's the price we pay for living in London.'

'Well, I am very sorry it is not Wiltshire we are looking out on,' Bella snapped.

'Oh, Bella, is that really worthy of you?'

'It isn't,' she admitted, blushing.

Now Westland took his turn at the window. He stared out for a while, sipping his wine. Then he turned back to the room, with a faint smile on his face. 'Mr Edwards has just come into the street. If Henry Ellis Margam had control of what happens next, I should end the evening as a hero. Instead, I am going out to confront him with'—he searched the room briefly—'this poker.'

'You'll do nothing of the kind,' Bella wailed.

Westland embraced her. 'Even a clumsy man with a poker is not entirely without menace, my dear.'

'Westland, if you love me, don't do anything so rash!'

'I haven't quite finished. The second part of my plan is that the Captain will run like the wind into Leicester Square and come back with a policeman.'

'Like the wind is good,' Quigley agreed. 'That part of it is very good.'

'Are you both mad? I will go out and face him,' Bella shouted, tugging at the poker end.

'You, for once, will do as I say. You will stay at the window and act as a witness to whatever ensues. Captain?'

'I'm your man,' Quigley grunted, hastily pouring himself a last brandy. 'Now then, sir. None of the old thrust and parry lark. Don't stand on no ceremony. Just lamp him with the poker before he gets his hands out of his pockets.'

110

The Battle of Orange Street was explained to
Constable Swain by the musician Hedley Hubison,
who had a God-given talent for getting hold of the
wrong end of the stick. Hubison had been sacked
from almost every pit orchestra in London for
quarrelling with the conductor. The rows he
created were of a very high-flown nature, to do
with interpretation of the score. They often took
place during the performance.

He peered into Swain's honest face, flecks of
spit at the corners of his mouth. A tall man, he
nevertheless stood on tiptoe in cracked patent-
leather shoes. His beard wagged.

'If you could just speak a little more clearly, sir,'
asked Swain.

'I was talking to Gough, the greengrocer, whose
child I am teaching to play the fiddle. Fiddle-
playing is nothing if not posture and the child is
as round-shouldered as—an exact comparison
escapes me for the moment—'

'Can we get on to what you saw, sir?'

'—because of course people think teaching the
fiddle is hack work. Well, not in the way I conceive
it, oh no.'

'You were talking to Mr Gough the
greengrocer,' Swain prompted. 'Then what
happened?'

Hubison pointed theatrically to Bella's door.
'Two men came out of that house, one a gentleman
known to me by sight, the other an ill-found sort of
fellow who ran away. He had a poker in his hand.'

'The one who ran away?'

'The other,' Hubison corrected. 'At which

111

Gough said to me, in a half humorous way—'

'Where was the third party?'

'Who? Oh yes. He stepped from the shadows, I imagine with the intention of remonstrating—'

'The cove with the poker was saying what, exactly?'

'There was great confusion,' Hubison admitted after a few moments' hesitation. 'As to what his exact words were, I cannot say, but in a general sense it was "have at you" and that sort of thing.'

'While brandishing a poker?'

'Brandishing,' Hubison mused thoughtfully. 'I'm not sure that brandishing is quite the word—'

'Waving it about, then.'

'As I said before, he is a gentleman.'

'Well, was he waving it or not?' Swain demanded.

Hubison blinked. 'The man with the knife—'

'This is the one who stepped from the shadows?'

'Well, yes. Yes, of course.'

'He had a knife, did he?'

'A very large knife.'

'A carving knife, no doubt. To go with the poker.'

'You are being facetious.'

'Possibly,' Constable Swain admitted.

'I really wonder what it is you policemen do to earn your pay.'

'Oh, you do, do you? What I want to know from you, Mr Hubison, is why this cove with the knife come to be wearing this around his neck?' He held out his meaty hand. Hanging from a stubby forefinger was a length of cord with a weight at each end. Swain had recognised these easily enough—they were exactly equal stubs of pie-crust

112

lawn edging. Terra cotta, but chunky enough for all that. He had something like it in his own back garden.

'Well,' Hubison muttered, 'they appeared as if from nowhere.'

Which was more or less what Molucca was explaining to the doctor across the river at St Thomas's. Attempting to explain. The livid bruise around his neck had played havoc with his voice box and he croaked like a raven. From time to time, his eyes crossed. Twice, to his great shame, he fainted.

Nobody in Orange Street had noticed the well-set-up toff who saw all this, walked into Charing Cross Road and hired a cab to take him to Chelsea and Cadogan Square. Nor did they hear—how could they?—how the man changed his mind and redirected the vehicle to Elm Park Gardens.

'You're the guv'nor,' the cabbie said.

CHAPTER TEN

'It is called a bolo,' William Kennett explained calmly, a glass of Bella's brandy at his lips. 'The gauchos of Argentina are very expert in its use. I have been practising on and off for several months. You whirl it over your head and let fly at the legs of straying cattle.'

'Do you have straying cattle in Chiswick?' asked Bella.

'Not in any great quantity. I have to admit it was a shot I couldn't repeat if you were to give me five years of practice.'

'But how did you know he was going to be in the street in the first place?' Philip Westland wanted to know.

Kennett waved his hand at Billy Murch.

'Sir William has gone away into Cornwall,' Murch explained. 'Judd stays in Cadogan Square, alone. I was giving the place the once-over in the manner of a standing patrol, as Percy Quigley would have it, when this Molucca came round to see him. Never got further than the front step. Instead, they walked to a pub called the Feathers. I followed and it was easy enough to get the gist of the conversation. Judd was telling his mate to get on with it. Orange Street was mentioned as the place where it had to be done and so forth.'

'Now why was that?' Bella wondered.

Kennett had an answer. 'Clearly, if Philip was to be attacked, he hoped you might witness it. Perhaps it was important you did witness it.'

'Billy?'

Murch shrugged. 'I don't know the gentleman. But if you ask me, he sees us as no better than heathen Chinamen. It's what you'd do to put the frighteners on the poor devils out there, so as to have your way of going on properly understood.'

Bella had to acknowledge the possible truth in this. Was Judd simply showing his strength in the way he knew best?

'You went home to alert Mr Kennett to the danger?' she asked.

'After following the other bloke home, yes.'

Billy Murch set down his glass and stood up, a tall and rangy figure with a natural grace. 'With your permission, I will hook myself out of all this and walk round to Fleur de Lys Court for a gab

114

with the Captain.'

Philip Westland jumped up and pumped him by the hand. 'Mr Murch, you have done us proud. We will continue here a while and then I and my friend Kennett will join you for a drink or two later.'

Murch's smile was almost affectionate, the kind an older brother bestows on an over-eager sibling. Bella walked him to the door. There she astonished and embarrassed him by seizing his bony shoulders and planting a soft kiss upon his cheek. 'That is to thank you, Billy. I fear there may be much worse to come before this business is all over.'

'You can be sure of it,' Murch agreed, his face brick-red.

*　　　*　　　*

When Liza Givens opened the door to Robert Judd in Elm Park Gardens she immediately took a step back, her hand at her throat. Let him think it was coyness if he liked but she was extra-sensitive to the look of a man, the signals he was sending out, as she had to be in her profession. Danger came off Judd like a wreathing smoke.

'Molucca ain't here,' she said.

'I know that. You're looking particularly fetching tonight, Mrs Givens.'

For a moment it crossed her mind that he had come for sex. Taking all things together, that would be the least worst outcome to his visit. 'I was just about to take a wet, Mr Judd,' she lisped prettily. 'Perhaps you will join me?'

'I came to explain something to you, dear lady.'

'Well then, I am all ears.'

'I will put it very simply. I have a large business venture in hand. You could say it is a turning point in my life. I won't trouble you with the details but something of a make or break nature. Do you follow me at all, Mrs Givens?'

'At every point, Mr Judd.'

'I was raised in a hard school.'

'As weren't we all? Will you not sit down for a moment?'

'I came to say goodbye.'

'Goodbye?' Liza asked, very startled.

'Just that,' he agreed.

'Then I won't see you again?'

'You never will.'

*   *   *

That same night, towards ten o'clock, Judd rescued Molucca from St Thomas's and drove him by cab to a chophouse in Artillery Row. It was in its way a refined form of cruelty—the injured man was relearning how to swallow and left his plate untouched. The bandage around his neck gleamed in the candlelight. On the other side of the table, Judd chewed and swigged ferociously. The way he ate explained his discomfort at the charity lunch in the City. Food was not the accompaniment to something else: it was primal. Away from prying eyes, Judd ate like a savage in a cave.

'You don't say what happened,' he said through a last mouthful of meat.

'I wish I knew,' Molucca whispered painfully, his fingers at his throat.

'Let me tell you then. You were bushwhacked. And how do you think that came about?'

116

'Someone ratted on me.'

Judd pushed his plate away and lit a dark brown cheroot. 'Your whore ratted on you.'

Molucca nodded mournfully. 'She'll pay.'

'That's all taken care of,' Judd said. 'Where's your knife, Molucca? Your famous Susan? I'll tell you where, you sorry sack of guts! You dropped it in the street and the police have it now. Which is bad news for you. Very.'

'What have you done, Bob?'

And Judd laughed, actually laughed. 'Did you give them your address at the hospital?'

'They won't treat you otherwise.'

'Then don't go back there. If you know of a deep hole in which to hide, I'd go this very night. And if I ever clap eyes on you again, even at a distance, even a glimpse of you on a passing train, you're a dead man. I hope all this is clear enough.'

'Is Liza dead?'

'Very much so,' Judd murmured, clicking his fingers to signal for the bill.

'You killed her?'

'Somebody did. Slashed her open with a very big knife. Like yours. Like Susan. I don't know who could have done such a terrible thing. I expect the police will have their own ideas about it, though.'

Molucca pushed back his chair. There were tears in his eyes, some of them from indignation, some—though he could not have phrased it this way himself—from unrequited love.

'All that time we had together in the East, Bobby, the scrapes we got into, the times I saved your arse? I've killed for you, I've taken the knocks for you. All that counts for nothing?'

Judd set down some coins beside his plate and

rose. 'It's business,' he said.

*   *   *

Liza Givens lay face-down on the carpet, her body sprawled on what seemed like a red cloak, spread from her hips as far as her shoulders. Captain Quigley observed how small her hands were, and how white.

'Her old dad was a railway porter, did you know that?'

He and Billy Murch were drinking Molucca's gin and smoking curious little black cheroots with a bit of stick in the end. It was three o'clock in the morning and the streets were utterly silent. Only once, an hour earlier, had they stiffened at the sound of boots on the pavement outside. It was nothing but a young man passing with a canvas bag of tools, a carpenter's trestle slung over one shoulder.

'He ain't coming back,' Murch decided. 'Not that you'd expect he would, neither.'

'A railway porter,' the Captain repeated, following his own train of thought. 'Could be found any night of the week in the back bar of the Wellington. A bad house. As a maid, she would be sent to fetch him home.'

Murch gave a huge yawn. 'Molucca didn't do it. She came down to the street with him to see him off. Calling after him to be careful.'

'If he didn't kill her, who did, Billy?'

'Some other heartless bastard.'

The slip of paper on which Robert Judd had written Bella's address was still on the black marble mantelpiece. Murch picked it up and left

118

his empty glass in its place.

'Offski,' he suggested.

They tiptoed outside in their socks and not until they were two streets away did they sit on the kerb and drag on their boots.

'For all her faults, she was a nice girl,' Captain Quigley muttered, probing with his tongue for a shred of tobacco.

Murch patted him on the shoulder and walked off into the gloom of what was promising to become a mid-morning pea-souper. Quigley blew his nose on his fingers and staggered to his feet. He was thinking of Liza Givens's father and the peculiar blue and mauve mottling on his face and neck. And the Wellington, where once the flash mob had gathered, now grown sadly ordinary. Ghosts, the Captain thought. This bloody city is full of them and that's no error.

*   *   *

William Kennett's house in Chiswick had been passed down through the family since 1772. Set back from the road and screened by trees, it retained (at any rate on the outside) an eighteenth-century suavity. Horace Walpole had dined there and in nearer times the artist William Hone and the statistician Chadwick.

Bella, whose mood was in any case nervy, was utterly dismayed by the interior. Books were piled in columns against the drawing-room wall and boxes of nondescript pottery shards jostled with rocks and fossils. On the exquisite little table where Kennett's grandmother was wont to preside over tea was a greasy iron clockwork engine and

119

the tools to mend it. Kennett's hands hovered but he could not bring himself to move anything and instead began erecting a shaky card table.

The light was dismal. Outside, a gently swaying fog obliterated all but the nearest features of the gardens and seemed to cast a yellowy shadow over the room itself. Every corner was in gloom. The silence that comes with fog was very marked.

'What is that smell?' Bella asked.

'Embalming fluid,' Kennett explained. 'I have offered to preserve Mrs Rogerson's cat, of which she was very fond.'

Just at that moment, Mrs Rogerson came in with tea. Bella was expecting a long-suffering and doubled-over skivvy and saw instead a woman hardly past thirty with a broad face and merry eyes.

'Murch is in the kitchen,' she announced to her master. 'He asks me to tell you Captain Quigley patrols the lane outside.'

'Will you tell Mr Murch that the threat of invasion is very remote?'

'You can tell him that yourself. He has a loaded gun by him meanwhile.'

Kennett stared. Bella's stiff back and pursed lips made him ill at ease. 'Tell him that is a damned impertinence on his part,' he said.

Mrs Rogerson was entirely unperturbed. 'I'll pass the sense of that along, shall I? He'll cringe like a dog, I don't doubt.' She nodded to her employer's guests. 'You'll find the tea not much better than hot water but that is the way he likes it.'

'An outspoken widow,' Kennett mumbled after she had left.

'You have kept her very quiet,' Philip laughed, the way men do. But the moment was ill-chosen.

120

Bella rose to pour the tea, which was indeed as pale as rosewater.

'Can we come to the point?' she asked, with far too much asperity. Because, she thought, we shall otherwise sink into a fog of our own. We shall give way to the fatuous and whimsical and end the morning playing with William Kennett's inventions, cribbed like small children in a world of make-believe.

These reflections disturbed her, all the more so for being apparently obvious to the two men. They added to an already foul mood. Mrs Rogerson's frank offhandedness annoyed her, the ridiculous tea annoyed her. Most of all, Philip Westland's passivity and good nature annoyed her. Last night, when they should perhaps have been closest, they had slept apart.

'We are here as a council of war,' he began, with a truly maddening deference, as if humouring a lunatic. It flashed through Bella's mind that what she would like to do most was to run up and kick him on the shins. When he saw the look in her eye, he examined the carpet between his boots, flushing slightly. My God, she thought, am I such a bully?

'Very well. Let us start with the poor woman Liza Givens. Judd killed her. Can we agree on that?'

'We cannot. There is no proof,' Philip pointed out. 'None.'

'But Murch thinks so,' Kennett replied in a low voice. 'It makes sense.'

'I also believe it to be true,' Bella snapped. 'But how can it make sense? What danger was she to Judd?'

Philip Westland answered, his good-natured

121

face stricken almost to tears. 'She betrayed him. She thought she was doing no more than gossip with an old acquaintance—Quigley—without realising that whatever she said would come straight back to us. If you like, we helped to kill her.'

'What an utter fool you are sometimes, Philip,' Bella said with far too much vehemence, feeling a dam burst inside her.

Without a word, he rose and left the room. Perhaps it would have been better if he had slammed the door behind him but instead it closed with a polite click.

'That was harsh,' Kennett said.

He seemed to expect she would go after her lover. But instead Bella flung herself into an occasional chair, making the joints wince in complaint. To his embarrassment, she covered her eyes with her hands as if about to burst into tears.

'Philip was in the right of it last night,' she confessed. 'All this has come uncomfortably close to home. That is what is making me so awkward. I do not like what has happened and have no clear idea what to do.'

'Has it occurred to you that we are dealing with monsters?'

'I am a writer, William. I can't work without looking for the monstrous in people.'

'The monster you are searching for in Judd seems to me to be quite apparent. He stands to lose a great deal. Unless and until he marries Mary, Sir William's fortune must escape him. What won't he do to prevent that happening?'

'Is he truly so vile?'

'He is following Sumatra rules,' Kennett

observed. 'That is, to do whatever is necessary.'

'Up to and including murder?'

'I don't think you have it yet,' William Kennett said. 'What happened in Orange Street last night was Judd's way of murdering you. By proxy, to be sure. Philip was completely in the right of it, though in a way he does not understand. The idea of attacking him was a way of warning you off. When that didn't work, something even more horrible happened.'

'This is very far-fetched.'

'Do you think so?'

'I could not write such a plot.'

Kennett looked at her with an expression on his face that hurt far more than outright contempt. 'If you will permit me to say this, Bella, whether you are a writer or not does not come into it. Judd doesn't know or care what you do for a living. You are simply in his way.'

'Doesn't he realise that this is London and not some woebegone shanty town or mangrove swamp?'

'He does not. There are millions at stake. Truly, millions. He would walk from here to Land's End on red-hot coals to get what he wants. This is not some social contretemps over the dinner table or a slight from a man you disdain. Nor is it an unwelcome review of a Henry Ellis Margam novel. This is war.'

She jumped up and began pacing, her heart in a turmoil. 'I have made a fool of myself,' she wailed, bursting into tears, something she had not done since she was a child. She was thinking of the little clockwork plot that animated the pages of the book she had so far completed. Whether Sir

William Skillane, the slum landlord and shipping magnate, secretly ate peas off his knife or dropped his aitches was entirely beside the point. He was not the story. Sumatra rules were the story.

At which point, Philip Westland came back into the room and, ignoring Bella's tears, seized her by the arm and drew her to the window.

Out on the lawn, two smudged figures stood stockstill in the fog. One was unmistakably Quigley. The other—head hung low—was Molucca Edwards. Somewhere along the way he had lost a wig and a bald pate made his head seem huge. A figure approached from the house— Murch. The three men set off in file, heading towards the stables, paying not the slightest attention to the drawing-room windows, where Philip Westland was disengaging himself from Bella's sobbing embrace and Kennett was running to the door.

*　　*　　*

'We will bring him into the house when he is ready,' Murch said through a crack in the stable door. His voice was calm.

'I think this is my property,' William Kennett blustered.

'So it is and we will bring him to you in a while.'

'Tell me at least how Captain Quigley came to capture him.'

'The poor bugger gave himself up,' Murch smiled. 'He is here to throw himself on your mercy.'

'Then let me speak with him.'

'Soon enough.'

Molucca sat listening to all this on a broken-back chair, his chin in his chest. Quigley stood over him with a handy length of iron railing, as much in awe of his surroundings as the prisoner himself. The stables were filled top to bottom with things William Kennett thought one day might come in handy, of which the iron bar was one of the lesser examples. At a quick glance there were more than twenty cartwheels, the condensing boiler to a small locomotive, a small mountain of cogs, timber of all lengths, nautical blocks and pulleys.

'Is the cove you work for a chandler of some sort?' Molucca asked in his new (and permanent) throaty whisper.

'Never mind that, mate,' the Captain rejoined. 'It's your pal Judd we want to know about.'

Molucca raised his head at last. 'He turned me off. As easy as kiss my arse. I have done him favours a prince would be grateful to accept. Go and lose yourself, he says. I'm telling you boys, that ain't easy.'

'Because of what's laid out on the floor round at your Chelsea gaff.'

'I never touched her,' Molucca said piteously. 'He did it, he told me as much.'

Murch pushed the Captain aside and put his face an inch from Molucca's. 'You haven't got the brains of a gnat, you poor bastard. That's why you're here with us and not up in the big house. Peaching on him isn't going to work. No court'll convict on what you say he said. So leave that out.'

'Leave it out,' Molucca agreed, forlorn.

'Take into account, Billy, he did give hisself up to us. Point in his favour.'

'As to that, Perce,' Murch growled, 'I'd as soon

125

maim him as speak to him. Put his eyes out with some handy bradawl. Or a six-inch nail. Which there are enough examples right underfoot.'

'That's a way of looking at it,' Quigley admitted. 'I see where you're going with that.'

'Oh, and I'd stand for it, would I?' blustered what was left of the old Molucca. But long experience of tight corners told him that in any fight he would get no further than the door.

Billy smiled. 'Yes, that's right,' he said, as though reading these thoughts. 'I'm in the mood to smash you up, Molucca. Can't get my hands on Judd but I have got you sitting there. Pass me that length of iron, Perce.'

'No, no,' Molucca said hastily. 'I gave myself up voluntary, didn't I? I have enough sea-time to get a berth and sod off out of it. Wasn't I at the docks this morning? But until this bloody fog lifts I'm a sitting duck. The police is after me. You know that. I'll tell you anything you want to know.'

'Captain,' Billy Murch suggested, 'step over to the kitchen and ask Millie Rogerson to brew us a cup of tea. Real tea, mind. He's going to tell us what we want to know.'

After Quigley left, Molucca seemed to perk up a little. Murch watched him with the same quiet smile.

'Fancy your chances a bit better now, do you?'

'Could give you a fight of it any day, mate.'

'Course you could. Big bastard like you. But you don't have the stomach for it. And for why? Because you're already beat. Coming home has done you no favours, Molucca.'

'And that's no lie,' the big man whispered, massaging his ruined neck.

126

'Now. If you was to tell me—which you have—that we shall see the back of you in a day or two—'

'Just watch my smoke,' Molucca promised.

'—then that might alter things. That might sit well, so to speak. But before you go, there's a lot you must cough about your mate Judd. Because I'd as lief kill you as wave you goodbye. Are you following this?'

'We're out of the same box, you and me.'

'No, no, no. I have spent my life scraping people like you off the sole of my boot. We're not brothers under the skin. So. I'll just tickle up your memory with this here iron bar, shall I?'

He swung the bar against Molucca's shins, getting in response a satisfying bull roar. The big man fell off the chair and rolled around the cobbled floor, cursing. He could be heard twenty yards away in the kitchen, where Mrs Rogerson had the kettle in her hand. She turned like a bristling dog.

'Be easy, girl,' Captain Quigley smiled. 'It's just Billy having one of his little chats. One of his little parley-voozes.'

The commotion was also heard in the drawing room. Philip Westland was at the window, watching the fog shift and slide.

'Is this how it's done?' he asked bitterly, as much to himself as anyone else.

CHAPTER ELEVEN

A man had once told Bella that if you were to climb a tree in Hyde Park you could look across

127

what appeared to be uninterrupted forest all the way to the Surrey side of the river. It was a trick of the eye but there were certainly more trees in London than its bitterest critics supposed.

But not in the grimy canyon of Shelton Street, where the only green rose out of the gutters at rooftop level as defiant tufts of grass and the like. During the night the week-long fog had lifted, though not enough to allow the sun to shine through completely. Instead, a strange diffused light reduced the sooty houses and wet cobbles to something like the effects of black and white photography.

Bella arrived at the little herbalist shop in a very chastened mood. She kissed Hannah Bardsoe on the cheek and shook hands with a cautiously attentive Charles Urmiston. 'You once promised you would be there if ever I needed you,' she began without any niceties.

Urmiston studied her with a faint half-smile on his lips. The parlour was scented with laudanum, for Bella had interrupted him in measuring out throat linctus into little brown bottles. Their tiny corks were scattered like acorns across the table. Hannah Bardsoe sat watching with her chin in her hands.

'I believe I did say that.'

'I am in trouble, Charles. Or in a better phrase, trouble has found me out.'

'Ho,' Hannah cried in a boisterous attempt to rally her friend, 'any expression but that, my dear! That is the way foolish green girls announce themselves to me out there in the shop when they've taken a fall.'

'Nothing like that, Mrs Bardsoe,' Bella said.

'Don't mind me,' she said. 'That was just my little jest. I'll leave you to chew things over with Charles, while I walks down into the Market for a cauli. Which if I haven't got a pound or more of good red country cheese that'd go with it, enough to make your heart ache for the old days, the simpler times we used to live.'

Urmiston escorted her to the shop door, kissing her goodbye as if she were off to an expedition up the Niger, even going so far as to pat her black straw hat down on her head.

'How lucky you are,' Bella found herself exclaiming gloomily. 'Was there ever a happier couple in all London?'

Urmiston did not reply immediately. Finding a cork that had rolled to the carpet, he replaced it on the table as lovingly as a child with a toy soldier.

'The story you have to tell me concerns the Skillane family, I don't doubt. I propose we hear it with a glass of Mousseux to hand. It comes from Rheims, the wine, but more nearly from the docks, where one of our customers has a son who works as a clerk. His job is to write off warehouse breakage and spillage. As a consequence we are all wine drinkers in Shelton Street nowadays. Crime, I have discovered, is an elastic quantity,' he added shyly.

'I don't disturb you from your work?'

'Never in life, though I must jump up to serve in the shop as need arises. Unless you would like me to put up the closed sign for a while?'

'The story is simply told, Charles. What I am after is your advice.'

'Then let us see what we can do.'

She started with the easiest thread. But even then
her tone was too dull, too maudlin. After only a
moment or so Urmiston reached and took her
hands in his, chafing them gently, his pale eyes very
attentive. There was hardly another man in
London who could have treated her so freely, a
thought that made her feel, if anything, worse than
she already did. She disengaged her hands and
busied them with lighting a cigarette, smoothing
down the chenille cloth, arranging the little corks
in columns of three. Although her account was
perfectly orderly, she was thinking of the coolness
that had come between her and Philip Westland
more than the story she was telling.

'I hope this is making sense,' she interrupted
herself nervily.

Urmiston smiled. 'I am managing to follow your
drift, I think.'

'I am very unhappy, Charles.'

'The bones of the matter first,' he suggested.

Bella nodded, licking her lips with the tip of her
tongue. They were dry as dust. She thought for a
second or two and then began to outline the
outcome to the Molucca Edwards story.

As she spoke, Molucca himself was beating
across the Bay of Biscay in a Dutch-owned barque
bound for Surabaya, a tarpaulin jacket flattened
against his chest and crotch, his seaboots filling
with steel-grey water. There was a sun up there
somewhere, not the one that warms the roofs of
houses by land, but a colourless disc, skating in and
out of long streamers of inky cloud.

Captain Van de Watering was on the afterdeck,

130

his shrill voice scolding the officer of the watch. This was the kind of vessel where the petty officers carried rattan canes: the elderly Van de Watering, two days out from Rotterdam, would like to have seen them used more liberally on what Molucca also considered a surly and recalcitrant crew. As for himself, relief and a chance to put himself as far from Robert Judd as possible made him a model able seaman.

His parting words to Bella in Chiswick had been that she would never see hide nor hair of him again, no, not for a fortune in gold. At the time he meant to indicate a self-imposed and mournful exile; but now, staggering down the lee rail in a cloud of spindrift, he found himself actually happy for the first time in months.

*   *   *

'He got away scot-free,' Bella explained sourly.

'Good riddance to him,' Urmiston observed. 'But a lucky fellow, all the same. He put his head into the lion's mouth and Murch, you say, took pity on him. How did that come about?'

'It was all very strangely done,' Bella said slowly, remembering Molucca sitting in William Kennett's preposterous drawing room, his feet bare, his boots somewhere in the stables as a pledge on his promise not to run. Prepared by Billy and the Captain, the questions Bella put to him were frankly answered, but terse.

'Yes, I know about the pearls, as who could not? Sir William will be long remembered in the East as the man who stole them from the Chinaman. For many out there, it's who he is. And all he is.'

'Have you ever seen them, these pearls?' Bella wanted to know.

'Once,' Molucca said, unable to keep the awe out of his voice.

'Has Judd ever proposed stealing them back?'

'Getting the girl is the same thing as getting the pearls. Mind, he wants it all. Kit and caboodle. Little Miss Mary, the pearls, the whole business.'

'And how will that come about?'

Molucca shrugged.

'There is a plan?' Bella persisted. At the same time it was beginning to annoy her that, in the corner of her eye, she could see Philip Westland slouched in an armchair, arms folded, like a sulking child.

'With Bob Judd, there is always a plan. You've already seen that.' He nodded sheepishly in Philip Westland's direction.

But if Philip was content to stay stubbornly silent, William Kennett could no longer contain himself. 'You realise that I will kill him long before he gets his hands on Skillane's daughter?'

'I wish you well of that,' Molucca said drily.

Because, after all, though he was slow and not from the same box as these grand people and their beautiful house, Molucca understood one thing very well. The lady was carrying the heavy end of the beam. And, naked feet or not, he could see freedom beckoning. He knew, as they did not, why his interrogation had begun in the stables with the two leery coves. They knew the score, spoke the same language, as the agonising throb in his shins could testify. Never mind that now. Give me another minute or two with this dozy lot, Molucca thought with some of his old cunning, and they'll

132

be lending me money and a change of linen.

And there things might have stood, he might truly have disappeared back into the fog, had not Billy Murch suddenly burst into the room.

'Has he told you all?' he barked without the slightest deference.

'Have you?' Bella asked Molucca.

'I thought I was talking among gentlemen,' he blustered.

Before anyone else could move, Murch closed his fist and punched him in the face with colossal force. Molucca's head rocked back and blood flew from his nose in a fine spray.

Bella flinched as if struck herself. 'Is this necessary?' she cried.

Billy pushed her aside and seized Molucca by the jaw. The big man's eyes were still struggling to focus.

'I gave you your chance, you toe-rag, and now I come in here and find you've thrown it back in my face. I put you on your word to tell them everything.'

'I told them all I know,' Molucca insisted, but without much conviction. 'My nose is coming up like a marrow, you bastard.'

Murch turned back to Bella. 'What is best, is for me and the Captain to take him outside, tie him to that tree out there and remind him where he stands in this game. You might not want to watch.'

'Isn't he doing his best?' Philip Westland muttered. They were the first words he had spoken for ten minutes.

Murch's glance could have turned water into ice. 'This is a man who's never met you, who sets off with a knife to cut you up and leave you for Mrs

Wallis to scrape off the pavement. No, Mr Westland, he is not doing his best. Has he told you about Linny? I see from your face he has not.'

*   *   *

In Mrs Bardsoe's tidy little parlour, the clock ticked a few dry seconds away. Charles Urmiston set down his glass. 'Linny?' he muttered, making the same mistake that Bella herself had made when she first heard the name, believing it to be a surname.

'That is Murch in a nutshell,' she said ruefully. 'Here were we three being fed unimportant titbits and he had already got out of Molucca—I don't know how—the key to the whole thing. The moment Murch mentioned the name, the poor fellow collapsed, just gave up the ghost. He had seen the chance of rooking us turn to dust in his hands.'

'But then, forgive me, who is Mr Linny?'

Bella nodded grimly. 'Just so,' she said.

*   *   *

In Cornwall, on a cliff path near St Just, with the Botallack mine chimneys half hidden by a high ridge of gorse and bracken, and nothing but the sea to the north and west, there was a miner's cottage built of boulder stone and scraps of wood. The roof was tarpaulin, painted nearly half an inch thick with ancient tar. The one piece of window glass in the place was cemented into the lee-side wall. The floor was unboarded, the walls black with peat. The tenant was a reckless girl called Linny

Trethewey. She had been promised the earth. Fate and Robert Judd had given her a child and this miserable kennel.

Things had started very differently, with a gentleman riding by. Linny's father had raised his back from hoeing to see his daughter run to fetch Judd a cup of cider. Watching them, it was all too clear that to them he might as well have been a gatepost or a dung heap. Linny, sixteen, was laughing, her hand to her throat. Suddenly, Judd reached down and hauled her up behind him. Her bare leg flashed, as high as her thigh.

'Now, Trethewey,' he called with his trademark insolence, 'wouldn't you like to see your daughter here taken into service, such a fine figure of a girl as she is?'

'That would be something,' Trethewey agreed with enough irony to split staves.

'You know Sir William Skillane's place?'

'Who doesn't?' Trethewey, greatly daring, spat.

' 'Tis a chance, father, that don't come by often,' Linny said.

'Some would say it comes by often enough to trusting maids.'

'Are we going to spend all day gabbing?' Judd asked. 'If you don't like it, pull her down and I'll be on my way.'

Trethewey shrugged. 'Mind yourself,' he told his daughter, as if she were the kind to pay the slightest heed. 'See her straight now, sir. And bring her back to tell her old dad what's afoot.'

'Shall come back in a carriage,' Linny promised, making Judd laugh.

That night, Albert Moss came round, as he did three or four times a week, to see his girl, the light of his life.

Trethewey was drunk, not spewing drunk but dangerous. 'She'm sunk,' he laughed when Albert asked after her. 'Less'n you want to go and win her back with all your great wealth, my dove.'

'Could go and put his lights out,' Albert proposed, but none too eagerly.

'That's right,' Linny's father crowed. 'Put his lights out in your manly fashion. What could be easier?'

Albert, with his harelip and reddened lumps for hands, his spine already twisted from clawing in the potato fields. A shilling a day labourer, already half lunatic. He fidgeted. 'Your daughter's a whore,' he decided.

'That, and some,' Trewethey agreed.

Judd took Linny to Boskeriss House, easily the largest property she had ever seen and as alien to her as might be Windsor Castle. None of the Skillane family was in residence and the place was being looked after by the housekeeper and her husband. All the rooms on the ground floor were closed up. Judd left the barefoot girl shivering in the corridor while he went to find Mrs Rowe and order hot water to be sent to the bathroom. The green bathroom, mind. Hot water and a bottle— make that two—of champagne. Meanwhile, Rowe might shift his fat arse and stable the horse.

The Rowes exchanged glances and said nothing. They were country people (she from Land's End, he from the offices of a tin mine in Lostwithiel) but they were not stupid. They had seen Judd come up the drive and they knew before she did why Linny was there with him.

'Is it Miss Mary's bathroom you spoke of?' Mrs

Rowe asked at last, very quiet.

'Just bring the water as fast as you can boil it and be damned with your questions.'

'If that poor whit has ever seen a bath afore it will be a miracle,' Rowe commented to his departing back, while planning how to catch a glimpse of her without her clothes.

And he was right: naked, Linny was brown with sixteen years of ingrained dirt. She sat in the bath with her arms crossed, watching Judd empty a jar of pale green crystals into the water and commanding her to kick. Alarming amounts of foam resulted.

'This ain't your bath I'm sitting in,' she accused him, playful but uncertain.

Judd smiled. 'No more than is that bed in the next room. When you finish here, you can stretch out in it like a young lady.'

'And where will you be?' she said with a child's attempt at archness.

'Use the little brush there. Scrub yourself pink. And wash the peat smoke out of your hair.'

An hour later, when he pulled away from her, he was surprised to see a flower of blood between her thighs. Linny was looking at him with darkened eyes, tears on her cheeks.

'I am not often the first,' Judd said, half to himself.

'Who is Mary?' Linny whispered. She pointed to a cross-stitch sampler framed and hanging on the gold and green wallpaper.

'What do you care?' Judd demanded, looking at her body without quite meeting her eyes.

*   *   *

137

'And he told you this? Molucca told you all this?'

Bella studied Charles Urmiston's anguished expression, in which disgust and compassion were mixed.

'He took a cottage for her in St Erth,' she continued. 'Bought her clothes, taught her manners after his fashion. Rode over to Trethewey's place and told him if he ever opened his mouth he was a dead man.'

'But the servants? Mr and Mrs Rowe?'

Bella smiled sadly. 'He is altogether very businesslike, Charles. Linny had never seen a three-storey house before and nor had the Rowes a five-pound note. After his own fashion, he got away with it. The Skillanes suspected nothing, least of all that poor innocent Mary. Then came the baby.'

She poured herself the last of the wine. 'She made the mistake of threatening to expose him as the father of the child. He turned her out of the cottage with the clothes she stood in and a sovereign. Her father would not take her back, this fellow Moss first belaboured her with a stick and then in a fit of remorse found her the place where she is now. Without Molucca Edwards—which is really to say without Billy Murch's way of dealing with him—we would not know any of this story, nor that she ever existed.'

'But now you have a chance to bring Judd's world down about his ears. And, I suppose, save Mary. That is your plan, I take it.'

'We have been discussing it in that light,' Bella said. 'Yes. But there is a problem.'

'Mr Kennett,' Urmiston guessed.

138

'How wise you are, Charles. William Kennett would stand to gain most from exposing Judd's infamy. Of course he would. But for him it is not enough. He truly wants to kill Judd. How it is to be done he cannot say. But he thinks it the only certain way to bring an end to the whole affair.'

Urmiston nodded. He stood, rubbing his thighs; and then walked into the scullery, where he filled a kettle with deliberate care. 'What you haven't said is the help you need from me.'

'Oh, nothing of a practical kind,' she called.

He was not a stupid man. He knew she had yet to reveal her true reasons for sitting there at his table, her head in her hands.

'Hannah will be back soon,' he said. 'I am making a pot of tea for all of us.'

'I don't know that Hannah—'

'Nonsense,' Urmiston said. 'You will tell her what's really troubling you and then she will tell me. That's the way it works best. Only then can I see what's in your heart, dearest Bella.'

*   *   *

The two women talked in Hannah's bedroom, the still air smelling very faintly of sweat and discarded shoes. It was the hour when the shop was busiest and downstairs they could hear Urmiston attending to customers with his trademark patience and courtesy.

'They come regular for their pills and potions—more than ever, now that Charles has tidied the business up, and me with it. But, like he says, it's not really their guts that are griping. Living is hard and tears come easy. My dear boy thinks we should

139

change the name over the door and call the place the "Chat Shop".'

'Have you ever asked yourself what it's all about, Hannah?' Bella asked in her tiniest voice. 'Everything, I mean.'

'Lord love you! And you the famous writer!'

'You have probably guessed what's troubling me. It is that very thing. I could write a story about all these recent commotions without leaving the house, without so much as thinking twice. Instead, I have made Philip Westland witness some terrible things—and put his life at risk besides. Do you remember when Charles went down into Cornwall because he could not stand it any more?'

'I think I do recall that unhappy time,' Hannah said drily.

'That is how I feel now.'

'Run away, is it? Is there no other way?'

'Mr Westland and I are at sixes and sevens over our future together. Which is a pale way of describing it.'

'Now there is very unwelcome news.'

'We have a chance of a place down in Wiltshire. I know he would make it perfect for us both. I love him, Hannah. I want him to be happy. But this, all this'—she waved her hand helplessly—'is holding me back.'

'This bedroom, do you mean?' Mrs Bardsoe smiled. 'Or is it London, the dirty old place? I daresay there's much in Wiltshire that is pretty to look at and people there that are kindness itself. But I'd be buggered if I could live among them.'

In spite of herself, Bella laughed.

Hannah wrinkled her nose. 'I don't say as how a quiet life isn't worth having. And, oh, won't I jump at the chance of a little whitewash cottage next the church when the time comes. But as I see it, those days ain't come yet. And that's the long and the short of it with you and Mr Westland.'

'You are right, as always.'

'I don't doubt there is more to it than I can tell. But what keeps you here is wickedness and how to defeat it. He understands that.'

'I have begun to wonder.'

'Then you must unwonder. I have met the gentleman but the once, the night you put your life at risk out there in Holborn. But I know adoration when I see it.'

Bella blushed. Hannah Bardsoe patted her hand gently. 'He has chose you, and you him. It's that old Henry Ellis Margam that's queering his pitch, is that it? Well, similar-wise, it does drive me to distraction sometimes to see my dear boy Charles acting like the Queen's physician to a bunch of old women without a pair of drawers to their name; but this here room is where we settle it, whenever it comes too much.'

So saying, she plumped up the pillows, helped Bella to her feet and smoothed down the counterpane. Her actions were brisk and businesslike but her cheeks were bright red.

'Running away won't help. That was my meaning. Shouldn't you give this Wiltshire place at least a lookover? Or speaking more frankly, Mrs Wallis my dear, closing the bedroom door on that old Henry Ellis for a few days?'

Bella resisted the impulse to hug her. 'Shall we share a touch of your best Martinique rum, Hannah?' she asked, pulling open the bedroom door.

'Oh yes, the rum! And if I hadn't forgotten that as a great peacemaker, too. Lead away downstairs. We'll see if we can't get Sir Charles Urmiston to finish his consultations and join us.'

He was waiting for them in the parlour, wearing his green baize apron and a strange felt hat that he put on when serving in the shop.

'Mrs Wallis has a mind to go down to Wiltshire for a few days, dearest,' Hannah lied briskly. 'For the holiday aspect of it. Same as we had them two days in Margate.'

'A capital idea,' Urmiston said gravely. 'I do hope Mr Westland will accompany her.'

'Well, would she go without him? I do declare, Charlie, sometimes you are as slow as some old snail. Wiltshire! Was ever such a romantic location? I am green with envy.'

Urmiston kissed her fondly. 'And do you know where Wiltshire is, my dear?'

'Why,' Hannah blustered, kissing Bella in turn. ' 'Tis where it always is, the month of September. Men, Mrs W! The questions they ask! And lost without women, if you follow my drift.'

CHAPTER TWELVE

Rain and more fog in London, but in Wiltshire a fine autumnal haze over the water-meadows. In the early morning the sound of marching feet as a full company of soldiers swung past, their red uniforms flowing like a ribbon against the green of the lane. Their helmets and belts were a dazzling white, the stocks of their rifles burnished like chestnut. As they marched, a grizzled old colour sergeant the size of a sentry box chivvied them along in a lulling, almost affectionate tone, like a man herding cattle. Yet-tchar! Chests out! Yet-tchar!

'A fine sight,' Bella exclaimed.

'They might say the same of you,' Westland replied. 'Not every cottage window they pass frames a beautiful woman; or at any rate, not a naked one.'

'This is the country,' she countered. 'Things are done differently here. We are closer to nature.'

She turned to face him and laid her arms around his neck. 'Does Kennett come today?'

'By mid-morning train.'

'I could wish him a thousand miles away. It really is a little corner of heaven here, Philip.'

'I concede nothing of my original idea, you understand—that we could be happy out of London. But I admit to being dismayed by the amount of walking about one has to do. You are nothing in this village if you haven't climbed that damn great hill out there at least once a week or strode along the river into Salisbury. Our neighbours are all perambulators.'

They kissed, skin to skin.

'You are intensely lovable. Have I told you that?' Bella whispered.

'You may have done. I live to make you happy, Bella.'

'But you don't like what I have made of myself.'

The pause before his reply was no more than a heartbeat or two; but for all that, it was too long.

'After breakfast,' he said, his lips against her neck.

As a consequence, this was a meal taken more or less in silence. After it, obedient to local custom, they walked; across the fields to a railway crossing, from thence down a narrow tunnel of blackthorn hedge more than a hundred yards long. Very disappointingly, it led into a stubbled field. To go on they would have to journey without paths to no obvious destination: it was more than Londoners could contemplate. They did what strangers to the country do and pretended to find beauty in a quite unexceptional view.

They were saved when Westland pointed out an ancient curiosity right in front of them—a quince, heavy with fruit, clinging to a fragment of brickwork.

'Were we to dig here roundabout, we should perhaps uncover a walled garden and in time the relics of a house. How cruel history can be.'

'This is maudlin of you, Westland.'

He picked her a green and ugly fruit. 'How I feel this morning, Bella,' he said slowly, 'is simple enough. It falls out like this. We can stay in Orange Street, or I will buy you another house in London. But I would be lying if I said I was happy to see you risk your life—or mine, come to that—now or ever again for Henry Ellis Margam.'

'Is that really how it seems to you?'

'Shall we say this: poets who write about waterfalls don't always feel the need to live under one?'

'If you love me, you must not try to change me.'

'I hope I have shown that,' he protested mildly.

'I do not coax these stories into existence, Philip, they spring up like serpents. You wouldn't have me as soft-headed as Cissie Cornford, for example?'

144

'I don't know that Lady Cornford is a useful comparison.'

'Why not? Isn't she a fictionalist in her own way? Isn't the biggest fiction of all the idea that life is merely wallpaper and servants, coats of arms and French chefs? And the tittle-tattle that follows from them?'

She nodded 'good morning' to a hunched farmworker coming along the field edge, a sack across his back. He touched the neb of his ruined cap without so much as glancing as he passed.

'I could not live that life and be happy,' she said, meaning Cissie Cornford's comfortable banalities.

'You intend to hunt this fellow Judd down, I take it?'

'I intend to prevent your friend Kennett from doing something utterly reckless. I don't ask you to join me. And I beg you to believe I make a very reluctant warder.'

Westland walked into the empty field a few paces. 'At least one thing can be settled,' he muttered distractedly. 'I could no more live here than fly in the air. Too much sky. And nowhere to hide.'

She laughed, in spite of herself. 'I didn't know you were in hiding from anything.'

'From things as they are.'

At their backs, a train thundered past, perhaps the one bearing Kennett. Philip had found a stick he pretended was of great interest. He swished experimentally. The stick broke in two.

'You will not marry me, I suppose?' he asked; and when she failed to answer, glanced over his shoulder with a wry smile. 'Never mind. We should walk to the pub and order something for Kennett to eat when he arrives. And if he attempts to walk from Salisbury by the river path, I shall wash my hands of you both.'

'How should he come then?'

'In a hansom, like Henry Ellis Margam on the way to the Garrick.'

'Philip, I am not completely cruel.'

'You mean that thing I said about marriage just now? Oh, that will come to pass one day. Like having to walk with a stick or taking the stairs one at a time. You will see.'

Though they held hands on the walk back, she found nothing to say that could break their mood. He left the quince he had picked balancing on a fence post, its glassy greenness winking in the watery sun. Some objects in the world are put there solely to provoke future dreams. This was one of them.

*   *   *

But it was not William Kennett who arrived in the village an hour later but Charles Urmiston. He had with him a brown paper parcel which turned out to be a cake from Hannah, a present he laid down on the sitting-room windowsill. 'Your surprise at my presence is understandable,' Urmiston began. 'I have taken William Kennett's place at extremely short notice—indeed, I had all to do to catch the train he designated.'

'Where is he?' Philip asked bluntly.

Urmiston looked about him, as if confirming to himself that this low-ceilinged room was indeed his destination. He had arrived wearing a ridiculous brown bowler that Bella knew without being told

146

had been bought from a second-hand clothes stall. His jacket was of the kind that cattle auctioneers might wear. This was Urmiston dressed for the country by Hannah Bardsoe.

'Sit down, Charles,' she said.

'I am flustered,' Urmiston confessed. 'There is some kind of war scare in London and the train was stuffed with military men. All talking very loudly and being amazingly free with their opinions. Salisbury in uproar. Leave cancelled, provosts everywhere. The fellow who fetched me here from the station says he has it from unimpeachable sources that the Russians intend to occupy Constantinople. I took him to mean imminently.'

'Can we leave such eventualities to the care of the Foreign Office?' Philip Westland snapped, far too briskly.

Urmiston flinched. 'I beg your pardon.'

'Better to tell us why Kennett has failed to turn up.'

'The two things are connected—Russian intentions and William's reaction. Or not his, but Robert Judd's.'

Bella and Philip sat and waited, lips pursed, watching Urmiston scrub his temples with his knuckles.

'I can only tell this story one way,' he complained feebly. 'I asked William to furnish me with a note but he didn't have the time.'

Philip lumbered to his feet and began pacing the carpet, his hands pulling at his hair.

Bella caught him by the sleeve and begged him to look for wine and a corkscrew. 'And you, Charles, please continue.'

147

'Very well,' Urmiston said, rubbing the crease across his forehead where the bowler had been sitting. 'Skillane's Black Sea fleet is British registered. In the event of a Russian occupation of Constantinople there might follow at the very least a blockade of the Dardanelles. You may look at me like that all you wish, Bella, but I am only repeating the scaremongering that has attacked otherwise perfectly rational people in London.'

'And these rumours have caused Sir William to stir himself down in Cornwall?' she suggested.

'There you have it,' Urmiston exclaimed gratefully. 'Sir William wires his anxieties to Judd in London, Judd is galvanised. He receives a second intelligence from a man called Kashvili—'

'How do we know all this?'

'Murch,' Charles Urmiston said with the greatest simplicity.

'And how does he know?'

'The answer is, I'm afraid, burglary. And, I suppose, theft. We have the telegrams.'

Philip came back into the room with a bottle and glasses, still wincing.

'Who is Kashvili?'

'Wait. No sooner has Judd received this second cable than he cabs post haste to Cook's in Piccadilly and books himself on to the Harwich steamer to Holland. From there he goes direct to the boat train at Liverpool Street, taking with him nothing but the clothes he stands up in. Kashvili is a man who stays at the Metropole in Rotterdam.'

'And?'

Urmiston shrugged. Westland fixed him with a stare. 'You have no idea who he is?'

'None. Judd sailed for Rotterdam towards

148

midnight of last night.'

'I have the most terrible feeling that you are about to tell us Kennett followed him.'

'Yes. By the morning service from Dover to Calais and thereafter by train. I can't say with what plan of action.'

'Taking Murch with him?' Bella asked sharply.

'Alone.'

The three of them sat trying to digest this. Then Urmiston remembered he had the telegrams in his wallet and fished them out, passing them to Bella, who skimmed the contents and passed them in turn to Philip.

'Kashvili is presumably an agent of the Skillane Company?' she asked.

Urmiston shrugged but Philip Westland nodded. 'It would seem so.'

'Then—and I may be missing the point somewhat—doesn't it make ordinary commercial sense for Skillane to instruct Judd to go to Rotterdam and find out what's happening?'

'You'll have noticed the Kashvili cable to Judd is in code,' Urmiston said.

Philip waved away the remark with a bitterly indulgent laugh. Bella looked at him. 'You think you could break it?'

'With patience, a child of ten could break it.'

'Then can we three try to match the ingenuity of a child of ten?'

Pencils produced, writing paper discovered in a desk drawer. The code comprised letters of the alphabet arranged in ten blocks of six. It read:

5KQJJY XFNQXX NHNQD2 9YMHMF SLJTKT
BSJWXM NUFLWJ JIHTSK NWRZWL JSYDP

'We can quickly discount the possibility that Kashvili's message contains ten nouns or verbs of equal length,' Urmiston proposed, with a nervous glance at the others.

'The groups might represent whole phrases or even sentences, if we knew the key,' Bella suggested.

Philip smiled. 'You are thinking of the commercial telegraphic code that the masters of merchant ships employ.'

'Kashvili is agent to a shipping company,' she pointed out.

'Maybe. He may be.'

'But it could be commercial code?'

'If so, there is enough here for a short story. No, I think this is what's called a substitution code. The letters represent other letters of the alphabet. Or at least, we might start with that possibility.'

Silent scribbling. Bella pointed out the presence of seven Js, which could indicate a vowel. Urmiston drew attention to the three numbers in the script and—after a few moments' reflection— the possibility that there were only two numbers, 5 and 29. More silence.

'Wait a minute,' Bella said. 'Suppose J to be a vowel. Then surely it can only be E or O.'

'If the first group is a single word.'

'But if not, what short English word ends in O?'

'Two,' Philip yawned. He lay back in his chair, hands folded across his chest. When Bella glanced at his worksheet, she saw he had written nothing but instead had drawn a heart pierced by an arrow.

'If the 2 and the 9 because of their juxtaposition might indicate 29, what does that suggest?' he murmured, like a weary don conducting a tutorial.

'A date, perhaps!' Urmiston exclaimed.

'Very possibly. And the 5?'

'Maybe some other quantity. Five million in bonds. Five days. Five gentlemen in seaboots. I don't know.'

'If you know,' Bella snapped at Westland, 'perhaps you would stop pouting and tell us.'

He sat up, as if forcing himself to take the problem seriously for the sake of his friends.

'Schoolboys amuse themselves with stuff like this, Bella, in the long afternoons otherwise devoted to Latin gerunds or the cape and bay geography of Britain. Suppose the 5 indicates a shift of five letters forwards or backwards, what does that first group spell, if anything?'

Bella bent her head over her scrap of paper, Urmiston likewise.

'FLEET,' they cried together.

'And the whole text?'

More busy scribbling. The new groups now read:

5FLEET SAILSS ICILY2 9THCHAN
NGEOFO WNERSH
IPAGRE EDCONF IRMURG ENTLYK

'Sir William Skillane seems about to lose an empire, but not to the Russians,' Philip Westland concluded. 'And it might be worth pointing out that the 29th is exactly five days distant. We now know what set Kennett off like a terrier.'

Urmiston stirred uneasily. 'I was not charged to come down here to tell you where your friend was. He asked me to order you both—I'm afraid that was his word for it—to return to London immediately and plan what to do about the Cornwall connection.'

'And what does that mean?'

'He would not say.'

'We are on the back foot every step of the way,' Bella said bitterly. 'A change of ownership might mean just that—the business passes by some legal instrument or other to Judd. It does not have to— in fact it would be stretching the point to make it— bear a more sinister meaning. The Skillane fleet is in danger of being bottled up in the Black Sea and will repair to Sicily. Where new ownership will be established.'

Westland took a turn to the windows and opened them on what was turning out to be an idyllic autumn day.

It was startling to Bella to realise she could read what was in his mind from the set of his back and the way his hands splayed on the sill. What she saw was dispiriting.

'This is exactly the problem, Bella,' he said slowly. 'Leaving aside the murder of Liza Givens, which we cannot prove Judd committed, what we have here is the correspondence of a very unlikeable set of scoundrels who nevertheless sail well within the law.'

'And?'

'For you to make more of it is to tell a story that may or may not be true.'

'To tell a story?' she repeated, cheeks burning.

'To invent. To do Margam's work for him.'

Her salvation came from an unlikely source. Urmiston first asked for coffee, if there was any to be had, failing that the strongest tea.

'As to Bella's dilemma, I have never yet known

152

her to tell a story that was not true. You discount Liza Givens and this other poor creature down in Cornwall because you have never met them. And you say, far too lightly, let the world roll on. Well, it's not good enough, Westland. It will not wash.'

'You are doing me the honour of calling my conscience into question, is that it?'

'Oh, for God's sake,' Bella shouted, storming from the room.

* * *

On the way back to London, the train stopped at Basingstoke for a scheduled four minutes, an opportunity some passengers seized as a chance to stretch their legs. Bella pushed past Urmiston's knees and opened the carriage door. He made no attempt to prevent her stepping down on to the platform. They had not spoken for more than an hour, and the atmosphere in the compartment was glacial.

Though a pale sun was doing its best, it could add nothing to Basingstoke station. The air was filled with steam and smuts; every surface was greasy to the touch. And—it struck Bella in her present mood—the landscape and the people in it were hideous beyond words. Enamelled plaques advertising cocoa, soap, proprietary medicines and washing products seemed to indicate to passengers that these things and their like were all they needed in life. In other places, prominent railway company notices told them what to do, where to go, how to avoid danger, how to walk down a simple flight of stairs, what was drinking water and what was not.

153

And all this while, sparrows flitted sardonically about under the platform canopy, feeding (or so it seemed) on what had leaked or been spilt from the human craving for order. The birds swooped and rose only a foot or so above the tallest beaver hats. Their tiny fallen breast feathers were swept up by miniature tornadoes, or blew like petals across the dusty floor.

Bella forced herself to acknowledge, as whistles blew and one by one the carriage doors slammed shut, that what she was experiencing was something close to hysteria. Honestly put, she could not give a damn about the arrangements of Basingstoke station, nor the people who used it. She was afraid of losing Philip Westland—which made it all the more absurd that the train was drawing out of the station without her, the guard hanging out of the last carriage, his green flag wagging. As he passed, he caught her eye, as if knowing full well what had happened and why she was being left stranded.

Henry Ellis Margam could have coped. A situation like this was meat and drink to him, though he would surely have transferred the scene to some more romantic location—a tiny halt in a Bavarian forest perhaps, or somewhere bleak and snowswept in Sweden. This man walking towards her now along the platform, breasting gouts of steam, his figure backlit by the sun, might be Robert Judd—vengeance in his heart, a silver pistol in his pocket, the blood of William Kennett on his hands.

In fact, standing in front of her was a hatless Philip Westland. Bella threw herself into his arms. 'Urmiston must think us both mad,' she sobbed.

154

'I was all for letting you stew. It was he who more or less bundled me out. May I propose tea? And perhaps an Eccles cake?'

He raised her head from his chest and kissed her full on the lips. 'Listen to me, Bella. Having once found you, would I ever let you go?'

CHAPTER THIRTEEN

The Hotel Metropole in Rotterdam lay halfway down a cobbled street of chandlers in the dock area of the city. Sentimental guests—and they were very few and infrequent—claimed they could smell the sea. What they actually smelt was tar and spice, mountains of Dutch potatoes—and a great deal of local sewage delivered into the river and sent back to its source by the stiff breeze that customarily blew across the estuary.

Right next door to the Metropole was a business selling uniforms, braided caps, solar topees, displays of gilt insignia and badges of rank. A printed card advertised that inside could also be purchased a patented double-lined tin trunk, suitable for the tropics and guaranteed termite-proof. Part of the window display was taken up by a sheaf of rattan canes and fly whisks, not at all arranged in a whimsical fashion but presented as the necessary and formal adjuncts of the East India trade.

It was not unusual for younger and more romantic customers to put on their new uniforms in the shop and then walk next door into the hotel bar as newly hatched third officers or assistant pursers. There they demanded the best in the house, clapped each other on the back, laughed uproariously, smoked luxuriously and offered complete strangers a drink. Many—especially those unwise enough to go upstairs with the Surinam whores who frequented the place—left in a sorry state, barely in a condition to find their ships, let alone their brand new caps.

Kashvili looked on them all with a father's fondness. His vantage point was a table in the shadows, where his piratical black beard put off all but the most delirious of these novitiates. The Georgian was one of those sprawlingly gross figures whose fat deceives the unwary, for when he stirred himself to stand up, he was revealed as a small but threatening mountain of a man. When Judd came into the bar, however, he hardly stirred, save for the flap of a hand in greeting.

'They have the innocence of children, these young gentlemen,' he explained. 'Papa puts up the money to send them to sea and the world beckons. I have yet to meet one who knows what he is in for.'

'Very touching,' Judd replied. But not so pointedly as to upset the Georgian, for Kashvili could be an awkward bastard when he set his mind to it. He had once been a ship's captain in the Skillane fleet, duties he discharged for the most part in a striped flannel kaftan and stocking cap, with felt slippers on his feet. Kashvili had been at sea since he was nine years old without ever serving under a captain in a navy blue serge uniform and brass buttons.

'My legs have gone,' he confided absently to Judd. 'What a terrible thing, to be old.'

'If all goes as planned, you can be carried about in a chair by Circassian slave girls.'

'That will be welcome,' the ruined captain said drily, running his fingers through his beard.

'Is it safe here?' Judd asked, looking around him into the gloom, alarmed momentarily by the clack-clack of billiard balls in an unseen annexe of the bar.

Kashvili laughed, reaching across the table and chucking Judd under the chin with a crooked forefinger. 'Can we be overheard? Of course! This fellow to your right is a poet. His subject is decadence. You see he drinks absinthe. Maybe he is listening. No, for sure he is listening! Is he safe in here? I don't think.'

The poet raised his shaven head from the table and, catching the glint in Kashvili's eyes, saluted sketchily and stumbled away.

'If he could only find the fare to Amsterdam, he would be among friends,' the Georgian explained. 'But he don't understand: everyone in here works at least as hard as the whores upstairs. Rotterdam! City without illusions! I like.'

Judd was barely listening, his face closed tight.

Kashvili folded his arms comfortably over his chest and peered. 'So, as to our present dealings, the captains are asking me how you intend to pull it off.'

'That is none of their business.'

'I have told them this.'

'You mean, *you* want to know how it will work.'

'Oh, please!' Kashvili protested, laughing. 'Am I looking so stupid? It will be done by trickery, blackmail. Poor Sir William, with his beloved knighthood and his dried-up wife. His ridiculous

157

house in Cornwall, and his tame bank manager.'

Warning bells rang in Judd's head. He leaned in across the table. 'What do you know of all this?'

'He writes to me of course. "My dear old Kashvili, my trusted friend!" You think he don't remember me? I gave him his start when he got back from the East. A fat old man with a nose for business and Kashvili, master mariner. Two thieves, Mr Judd. Don't you got that expression in English, as thick as two thieves? I think so, yes.'

'What do you want?' Judd asked, his throat dry.

'I want the pearls.'

Useless to ask which pearls: the Georgian's smile was all-knowing.

'All that will come to pass.'

'You don't got them with you now?'

'Are you mad? They're still at the bank in Cornwall. I've told you this.'

'I want,' Kashvili said simply.

'All in good time,' Judd countered, feeling sweat run down his spine.

'We get proper valuation, maybe here in Holland and then Kashvili get his sweetener.'

'There is time enough for that,' Judd repeated.

'You think? Last week, Sir William writes me big letter. "Kashvili, what is going on? You understand the human heart. Do I got enemies in this crazy world? Nice old man like me? What should I do to sleep happy? Tell me please."'

'And what did you reply?'

The Georgian shrugged. 'When you get the girl, you get the business. This he understands. We all understand. You hang the old man by the heels, his money falls out of his pockets. Not all, but enough. Then, when he die, you got everything. Maybe you

158

want it should go a little faster. What is this to Kashvili? It's business, he says to his pillow. Just business.'

'Then what is the problem?'

The Georgian examined his guest with unsettlingly feminine green eyes. 'The problem, my friend, is the lady with her throat slashed. The London lady you murder.'

'Molucca!' Judd divined at once.

'He came here. I find him ship. Nice ship. Before he goes, he wants to tell me story about'—he clicked his fingers impatiently—'about Mrs Givens, yes. The poor lady.'

With surprising speed, he reached across the table and seized his companion by the shirt-front and lifted him halfway out of his seat. Though he spoke in a whisper, his breath roared in Judd's face. 'You get rid of Sir William just like you plan, everything nice. And then come the police and arrest you. Then they hang you! That's the problem, Mr Judd.'

He threw the Englishman back in his chair. 'Soon enough, everything goes back to what it was. Sir William has had a bad scare. He walks on the beach, thinks about business. Two, three days he walks, maybe a week. He don't shed no tears but he asks, "Who else was in on this? Who can I trust any longer? I thought I got friends and this new shit shows me I don't got none. Better I make other arrangements, marry my girl to a Scotchman with a castle, something like that. And for his part in all this other thing, Kashvili I kill. My eight captains I keep, maybe. But Kashvili, who call himself my friend, him I kill."'

'That won't happen,' Judd said, none too

certain.

'You think? That old man is cunning like mountain bear. You think he sits in his house all day doing this?' He had not the word for it and mimed knitting with his thick fingers.

'If the police are after anyone, it's Molucca,' Judd said impatiently. 'They do not suspect me.'

Kashvili sank back into the shadows, his fingers at his beard again. 'You are big fool, Mr Judd,' he whispered softly. 'Tell me, please, what is doing the Englishman upstairs, a Mr Kennett? Has he come to Rotterdam to inspect new harbour?'

'Kill him,' Judd said instantly.

'But I like him,' the Georgian objected.

'Go upstairs and slit his throat. If you don't want to do it yourself, find someone who will.'

'I think you mean this,' Kashvili yawned.

'Of course I mean it. What's stopping you?'

'Yes, what can it be?'

'We are partners, aren't we?' Judd protested.

'Well, about this, I tell you something. I have nephew, my sister's boy, nice young man. He ask me once: "What is secret of long and happy life, uncle?" I tell him: Vassily, you have always to see around corners. Very important. You understand, Mr Judd?'

'We have a deal,' Judd said, his face white.

'We had a deal, maybe we still got a deal. But now, like I just tell you, we got a problem.'

'How did Kennett know he would find me here?' Judd asked, perplexed.

'That's not the problem,' Kashvili said. 'We tweak his nose a little, he tells us his story. The problem is, how much Sir William knows. You want to get rid of him. He want to get rid of you.

160

Maybe. Killing the whore was very stupid thing to do. Killing Mr Kennett could be worse. You don't think?'

Judd rose and pushed back his chair with enough force to topple it. For his part, Kashvili lit a cigarette, making enough blue smoke to wreathe his head, his beard and his unblinking eyes.

*   *   *

William Kennett really was upstairs. When the door to his room opened, he was sitting on the bed. In his hand was a toy of a revolver. He was expecting Judd and seemed utterly disconcerted by the figure blocking the threshold, roaring with laughter and facing him down with nothing more threatening than a chicken leg.

'Don't hide up here, English,' Kashvili bellowed. 'Come and drink. Your friend Mr Judd has gone.'

'Gone? Gone where?'

'He don't like the Metropole any more than you. Put your little gun away, Mr Kennett. Wrong to say you are among friends, but I don't got no bad intentions towards you. I swear.'

'I came here to kill Robert Judd,' Kennett said, greatly vexed.

Kashivili slapped his thigh with delight. 'And I come here to rob him of what he robs from Sir William. Maybe kill him, who knows? You play cards, Mr K? We go downstairs and play some cards.'

'Judd first.'

'Like you say in your country, the bird has flown. And how he wish he could fly, that bastard. You bet. You want Mr Judd, you must look in Cornwall,

161

I think.'

'He's gone back to England?' Kennett asked.

'For sure!'

When he saw the crestfallen look on Kennett's face, he burst out laughing all over again.

'Molucca tell me all about you. Nice house. Nice friends. Plenty money but very shy. You only got one problem in otherwise happy life—Miss Mary.'

'He will not get her,' Kennett warned.

'And that's why you bring your little pop gun to Rotterdam? Maybe you kill him when I have finished with him. But not today.'

'Today, if it's still possible.'

The smile vanished slowly from Kashvili's lips, as if the big man was at last noticing something about Kennett he had previously overlooked. He threw away his chicken leg into a corner of the room and pointed a greasy finger. 'That,' he said with great deliberation, 'would be big mistake.'

'It wouldn't help you, certainly.'

Kashvili blinked, as though it was the bed that Kennett sat on that had spoken with such impudence; or the wash basin and jug. 'You are long way from pretty house in London, Mr Kennett,' he said slowly. 'So don't talk stupid at me.'

'If I find him today, I will kill him. It's what I came to do. I'm not interested in anything else. Do what you like about all the rest of it. But now get out of my way.'

'Maybe you don't sleep so much last night. Maybe you're hungry. Maybe you're a little bit stupid, don't listen so good. This is not about pretty virgin girl with maybe secret moles somewhere nice, Mr Kennett. This is about money.

162

Big money.'

'There is no money in it big enough to stop me.'

Kashvili sighed and wiped his hands on his shirt. 'Now you don't think straight. I got no time for dreamers.'

'I'm warning you. Get out of my way.'

It seemed that far from doing that, the Georgian was about to advance further into the room and tear him limb from limb. Kennett perked up the pistol.

Kashvili looked affronted. 'You don't got no manners,' he said. 'Now I got to be shitty with you.'

Kennett squeezed the trigger. He was aiming low but the Georgian fell back through the open door and into the corridor like a fallen tree.

*   *   *

'You killed him?' Westland cried incredulously.

'I hit his leg, I think. It was all very sudden.'

'And the pistol?' Billy Murch asked.

'I can't remember. I didn't have it at the train station. I threw it away, obviously, but as I say—' Kennett looked at each of them in turn. 'He is a very big man. I was expecting blood and so forth but there was very little of that. I jumped over him and legged it. Ran. Some people followed to begin with but in time they gave up. I hit upon the location of the station by the purest chance.'

'Well, sir,' Murch said with an encouraging smile, 'it seems to me you have come out of it very fair. For a beginner, so to speak.'

And really, what else was there to say? It was gone one in the morning and Kennett had only been back in London four hours. He seemed, as

163

well he might be, only half awake—and more than a little bit shame-faced.

Westland threw up his hands despairingly. 'You go to Rotterdam, you stay three hours and you shoot the wrong man. I wish I had your genius, William.'

'Fortunes of war, Mr Westland,' Murch said loyally. 'It happens. I've seen it before.'

'In the Crimea?'

'There it was more common than not.'

Kennett raised a weak smile and pumped Murch's hand. 'I do feel a bit of a fool, all the same, Billy.'

They waited until Murch had left and then Philip pointed a finger at his friend's face. 'No more, William,' he warned. 'You were not made for the role of assassin. No more guns. No more romantic gestures. We will bring these people down, but in a more orderly way.'

'By appealing to their better natures, I suppose.'

'Don't sulk. And don't scowl.'

'Why did I stay in that bedroom when I knew he would come? When I knew he was downstairs?' Kennett burst out.

'Because you placed love above hatred. Because you are no use to Mary in a Dutch jail. And because,' his friend added gently, 'she would never have understood. Chin up. Tomorrow you will find your mood much improved.'

'What has happened?'

'It is late. I shall sleep here tonight, with your permission, and in the morning we will go to Orange Street. We have been dealt the Borodino.'

'Tell me what has happened. Tell me now.'

'Tomorrow,' Philip murmured.

Kennett's housekeeper, Millie Rogerson, had the pleasant habit of eating biscuits in bed. Her wonderfully full and rounded breasts were scattered with crumbs and—as though these did not weigh them down enough—she dragged Murch's head to join them. 'Did he really shoot that man, Murchie?' she asked.

'The little gun he took with him could be put to better use starting foot races. But it was a bold stroke, all the same.'

No one before had ever called him Murchie; and there were other aspects to Millie that were even more startling. It had been a long time since Murch had shared a bed with someone so young, but that was not it either. None of that love talk about her, nothing that was coy—and absolutely no word about the future or what it all meant. Murch was (though he could not have phrased it this way) entranced.

'What happens now?' Millie asked.

'Cornwall. You could come too.'

'I never been on a train and have no wish to. And what says you have to go, either?'

'Come on, Millie,' he replied uncomfortably. 'I have to. Else, left to themselves, who knows what mischief they will all tumble into? I bet you have been on a train at that.'

'Never! Look at Rogerson. He'd never been on a bus, even. And then one ran him over. I've led a very sheltered life. Until I met you, of course.'

'Well, as to that, I had no idea what women were really like until you and me crossed paths.'

Her laughter was silent but had the effect of shuddering her breasts against his face. She tousled his hair. 'You don't want to leave them to it and stay here with me?'

He raised his head, kissed her lips and stared into her face. 'I want you to be here when I get back.'

'Got plans for us, have you?' She knew she was pushing him into areas he did not like to go and was very surprised when he answered.

'Yes,' he said.

'Well, if you get yourself killed, don't come back here looking for sympathy.'

She slid down the bed and wrestled him playfully on top of her. Murch, who knew all about the sabre and could drop a man at up to four hundred yards if the rifle was true, found his heart was banging fit to bust. Making love to Millie was like opening a door at the top of a five-storey building and falling out into the void. Falling out and not crashing, but flying. Answer me that, he asked himself.

CHAPTER FOURTEEN

In Cornwall, Sir William had exchanged the luxuries of his morning bath in London for a more austere regime. He still rose at the same hour but it was his Cornish habit to pull on broad linen trousers and a thick Guernsey sweater and walk down the hill to the beach. Men that he passed— men in the style of Kashvili, hardbitten sailors— rose from the mending of their nets and knuckled their foreheads or simply gave him the steady stare: he never acknowledged their presence.

Once at the lap of the tide, he waded out up to his hips and washed his face and scrubbed his hair, adding a particularly gross finale to these ablutions by taking in water through his mouth and blowing it out through his nasal passages. Then, dripping wet, he retraced his steps, entering the house through the front door, where his butler stood with a towel. In his hand was a second cloth with which he erased Sir William's footprints as the great man tramped upstairs. At a suitable point in the morning, his clumsy bathing costume was retrieved from the floor, washed and flogged free of salt and set to steam in the dungeon-like kitchens.

'And if he don't kill hisself of cold one of these days,' Connie Swift complained savagely, rinsing the sand from the Guernsey sweater with bright red fingers.

'My dad see'd him at high tide a day or two back. The rip tore the kecks clean off his limbs and left him naked in those parts. A spout on him like a donkey,' her friend Ada added.

'Ho! And much use that shabby old thing will be when he's got the double pneumonia. I wish.'

Skillane seldom left the house other than to bathe. Like a man with nothing on his mind but the pleasures of a retired country gentleman, he was supervising the creation of a library from one of the downstairs galleries, to which end he had bought several hundred books, sight unseen. They had come by cart from Penzance, along with various nautical memorabilia—the binnacle of the steamship *Orrin*, run aground at Whitesand Bay, an engraved telescope from the brigantine *Etoile*,

167

lost with all hands at Nanjizal, and so forth. Skillane was buying history.

The truth was that he was happier in Cornwall than ever he could be in London. Boskeriss was a cold and miserable house as it stood now but there was something about its unforgiving bulk that pleased its owner. Choosing wallpaper in Cadogan Square could not compete with digging out an entire hill behind Boskeriss to lay the grounds to lawn; or, as now, fitting out an otherwise nondescript space as a panelled library, complete with false loft.

'With what purpose?' Mary Skillane asked of the loft. It was being built in sections under a canvas shelter erected on the terrace. Some of the completed frames were already indoors, lending the air a healthy sweetness.

'I am having a ship's model built of the vessel once named after you,' her father replied. 'The work is being done by the two brothers Morrison. When it is finished, we must take out that window to get the ship into the room at all. And then we shall boost it into the loft, all sails hung out to dry, so to speak, every detail truthful to the original. The masts are nine foot high, to give some indication of scale. And all this I do for you, Mary.'

'I barely remember the original.'

'And how could you? She ran against the rocks at Porthloe Cove when you were five. Smashed to pieces in under two hours. As fine a ship as ever swam and of the seventeen of us aboard, only three survived. I have never seen such hateful seas as that day.'

'A lesser man would have been broken completely,' Mary said in an entirely mechanical

168

way, for this was how the story was usually concluded.

Skillane looked at his daughter with a surprisingly gentle reproach in his eyes. 'You find me foolish, I don't doubt.'

'I have not said so.'

He picked up a curl of planed wood from the floor and twiddled it in his fingers. 'Your mother says I am a cruel man.'

'No!' Mary cried in anguish, putting her hands over her ears. 'You must not talk to me about such things—about anything that touches how any of us thinks or feels! It solves nothing.'

'The *Mary Skillane* was my first and last attempt to set aside the past,' he continued, as much to himself as to his daughter. 'I have never been more proud of myself than the day she floated. We had a village band to play and there were fireworks—a great many, with rockets and such. You were a child, hardly more than a baby. We slept aboard that night. No masts, not a scrap of rigging, the very deck uncaulked. This was when we lived in a three-room cottage over to Falmouth.'

He walked to the window and looked out on to the men digging with pickaxes at the end of his lawns.

'You won't remember that either. But your mother does. They were happier days. Yes, indeed. Robert Judd comes down by train tomorrow,' he added, as though wiping the slate clean of such sentimental gush.

'And what is that to me?' Mary cried, as piteous as any seabird.

'I should think a very great deal.'

'I would rather kill myself than see his face

again,' Mary said.

'Words I have heard often enough before. If you were a man—my son, I mean—I could explain the situation better.'

'Were I your son I would pistol Mr Judd before he destroys us all. I am not stupid, father. He intends your ruin.'

'Of course he does. Well, what should I do? Should I pistol him?'

'Yes,' Mary said with vehement simplicity.

There was a tap at the window and the master carpenter peered in, a short man with a purely white beard, set off by alarming black caterpillar eyebrows. Skillane glanced, nodded. He turned back to Mary. 'I have never been bested by another man, nor shall I ever be. I might have done more to make you and your mother happier but that is quite another story. One that we shall reflect on at our greater leisure, I don't doubt. That is Hargreaves at the window, Mary. I must give him his orders.'

'There is a gentleman in London,' Mary found herself confessing in a rushingly tremulous voice.

Her father held up his hand. 'One step at a time,' he muttered.

'But I have something to say! This gentleman—'

'I know what you wish to tell me, but it must be for another time. The loft goes in today, for tomorrow the Morrisons are bringing the *Mary Skillane* by cart from St Just. That matters more to me than the arrival of Robert Judd. By a long chalk.'

'You will not hear me out?'

'God's teeth!' Skillane roared. 'Cannot you see the rest of my days here hang by a thread? Is it too difficult for you to understand that this weekend and the party your mother intends for me is like a black waterspout on the horizon? If I am to outsail it, do I not need all my wits about me?'

'Then what is this nonsense with a loft and a toy boat?'

Sir William's expression hardened into loathing. 'What you call a toy is a reminder of the man I should like to have been and the son I never had,' he said, turning his back on his daughter and reducing her tears to a single cry of anguish.

*　　*　　*

It was the morning after William Kennett's return from Rotterdam. In Bella's drawing room, Captain Quigley was reporting on his standing patrol in Cadogan Square, where he shared the nightwatchman's sausages and made a bob or two on the side matching pebbles tossed into a bucket. The nightwatchman was a ruined old sot called Thursgood, who had once been handy with his fists—enough to take on in his day the Dublin Mauler, who knew as much about Dublin as any Birmingham navvie, which is what in truth he was.

'Can we just get to the point?' Bella asked. Quigley nodded and flourished his cheroot. In his short and inglorious career as a soldier he had once been left as an unloved and unkempt recruit to stand guard over a haystack for two days and two nights without food or drink. Cadogan Square was by comparison packed with incident.

'Mr Judd comes back last night. Mid-morning, puts up a few necessaries, not many, enough for a small bag. Slings a canvas gun case over his shoulder, sets off for sunny Cornwall.'

'We know this for a fact?'

'Followed the gentleman to Paddington,' Quigley asserted. 'Saw him buy his ticket.'

'Did you see him get on the train?'

'He had a sharpener or two in the buffet and some sort of meat pie. Then, like I say, he sets off. If you want to be exact about it, the train left with him inside it. First-class carriage, a clerical cove as travelling companion. A bishop, maybe. Beard, eyebrows, hyena laugh and so forth. Improving book to hand. Penzance mentioned. My duties completed: returned to aitch-coo for further orders. No thanks required. The honour of the service is all.'

'Billy Murch is in the pub across the road,' Philip Westland added. 'Take a wet with him while we confer, Captain.'

Quigley nodded but, reaching the door, turned back. 'A word to the wise. You might want to keep up the watch on Cadogan Square. I can have an intelligent boy there inside the hour.'

'To what purpose?' Bella asked.

'I take it we're on a war footing,' the Captain replied with not a little asperity. 'He can't run a proper campaign down there in the land of the pasty, I shouldn't have thought.'

'Who is the "he" in that sentence?'

'Both. Neither Sir William nor his mate Judd can afford to give up Cadogan Square entirely, I shouldn't have thought. Gone today but here tomorrow, so to speak. After all, London is the capital of crooked dealings. Connections by sea and rail to all parts of the continong and beyond. Not to mention—'

172

'A shilling a day for the boy, then. Can he read and write?'

'What, on a shilling a day?' the Captain protested jovially. 'Can't do neither, but runs like a whippet. As good as a telegram for his promptitude.'

'Very well. He reports each night to Mr Urmiston in Shelton Street.'

'Mr Urmiston to command the rear party,' Captain Quigley nodded approvingly.

'Duties he will share with you,' Westland added, falling into the military way of describing things.

Quigley goggled. 'I'm not coming with you?'

'You are not,' Bella said, very bluntly.

'Well, there's a turn-up for the book and no mistake!'

But Westland had the knack of putting this demotion into a context Quigley could understand. 'You are forgetting, Captain, that it is upon you that the safety of this house and the one at Chiswick depends. We are not going to Cornwall for an entire campaign—say in the way Napoleon went to Egypt—but as a raiding party. What muffins we would look if our base of operations was meanwhile left unguarded.'

Quigley chewed his moustache for a moment or two, enormously upset. 'And Billy? How does he fit in?'

'That's to be decided,' Bella said. But the guilty look in her eye settled it.

The Captain wiped his mouth with the back of his wrist. 'Well then,' he barked, his eyes popping. Making an extravagant salute, he banged out. He did not cross the road to the pub but set off for Fleur de Lys Court, his normal slouch replaced by

173

a straight back and swinging arms. His intention was to look martial but there was something faintly lunatic about him to those he passed. He realised this himself (and in any case the old hip was playing merry hell). Before disappearing from view, he turned and cocked a snook to whoever might be watching from behind Bella's curtains.

'Oh dear,' the kindly Philip Westland sighed.

*   *   *

William Kennett arrived ten minutes later. He had been promised a surprise and was given it the moment he stepped into the drawing room, in the form of an envelope handed to him by an attentive Bella. It was a letter posted in Penzance three days earlier and the envelope contained two sheets of stationery. One was a wildly written (and in places misspelt) invitation from Lady Skillane to join a weekend party to celebrate Sir William's sixty-fifth birthday. She was sure Mrs Wallis might not wish to come out of London for anything so 'triviall', though the weather was very 'clemment' and a display of fireworks promised. 'Nota benne', Mrs Wallis was on no account to judge the gardens as the finished article. Oh, and the majority of the guests were but simple Cornish folk. They had manners (some of them) but no breeding.

The second sheet was from Mary Skillane. Addressed to Bella, it was clearly intended for William Kennett's eyes.

'I add to my mother's invitation my own fervent wish that you will accept. I cannot tell you by how much I long to hear news of London and all who are dear to me there. You may ask why this

174

birthday fete is taking place in Cornwall and not Chelsea. It is a question that has caused me similiar perplexity. But, come! I beg you. Yesterday they were fishing for pilchards in Carbis Bay and I recollect how much that once interested you. MLS.'

'You will go?' Kennett asked, hardly able to control his voice enough to ask the question.

'I have sent a telegram of acceptance.'

'We shall all go,' Philip Westland promised. 'To Cornwall, that is. I can't imagine you and I will be specially welcome at Sir William's table, William, though we can surely promise him fireworks.'

'Is Judd there?'

'We have Quigley's assurance that he set off by train for that destination, yes,' Bella confirmed. 'Carrying, I should add, a gun case.'

'Sir William has rabbits,' Westland murmured, by way of explanation.

His friend nodded absent-mindedly and re-read Mary's note. And then fell to chewing his lip. 'This places you in very great danger, Bella.'

'I shall be slow to encourage any moonlight walks or trips around the bay,' she smiled. 'With these provisos, Philip was happy for me to accept the invitation. Not all Cornwall can be homicidally inclined. They live under the same law down there, I believe. According to Mr Urmiston, who knows the area a little, the people are too self-absorbed to be dangerous, except to each other.'

'You are not walking into a trap?'

'My dear William,' she protested. 'The alternative is that this thing descends to something far worse. Let us go and wreak havoc on all Judd's schemes and stratagems.'

175

'And how will we do that?'

Philip laid his hand on his friend's sleeve. 'We must get to the girl Linny and her child before Judd does. And then produce the evidence at the right moment. That is the key. More than the murder of Liza Givens, that is what will undo him. It hurts me to say so, but it's how the world wags.'

'And the effect of all this cheap theatre upon Mary?'

Philip was about to say something but Bella signalled for him to be quiet. She turned back to Kennett with glittering eyes. 'Will she be made to look a fool at the dinner table? It's possible. But perhaps I think more highly of her love for you than you appear to do. She needs to know the truth about Linny and the child. In a thunderstorm, it is better to be out in the open. Hiding under a tree is very poor counsel.'

'Do these revelations have to be made in public, though?'

'Where else, for God's sake?' Bella asked, very angry indeed. 'Have you so little confidence in her? Such small regard for the truth? You talk about cheap theatre. Is Miss Skillane merely your china doll?'

Kennett blushed. He took a turn on the carpet, pacing up and down a few times, his face bright red. Bella jumped up and poured herself a brandy, her hands shaking on the decanter. There was an awful silence, broken only when Bella picked up the Bradshaw and flung it at the wall.

Kennett bit his lip. 'We take Murch with us?' he asked in a tiny voice.

'He is across the road, waiting on our orders.'

'And who commands us?'

176

'I do,' Philip said in a firm voice. 'Without that understanding, we do not go at all.'

Kennett combed his hair with his fingers. 'I do not say it must come to guns and bullets—'

'I am very pleased to hear it.'

'—but if it does?'

'If it does,' Bella interrupted, 'we shall have failed completely. We get rid of Judd, we save that poor girl he so casually ruined, and later, when we have united Mary Skillane with the man she loves most in the world, we turn our attention to the shortcomings of her father.'

'Nothing could be simpler,' Philip agreed, though with enough irony to stun an elephant.

'I should apologise,' Kennett said to Bella.

'You should thank your lucky stars you have a friend in Philip Westland, who would probably rather pick oakum than make this excursion, much less appoint himself the captain of it,' she snapped. Then she relented and opened her arms to Kennett, who came towards her gratefully.

Philip smiled. When he was invited by Bella's glance to join them, he did. The three of them stood in front of the fireplace, clasping each other like children, which was how Mrs Venn found them when she came in to ask what arrangements her mistress would like to make for lunch.

Kennett disengaged himself. 'I think you have met my dearest friend Miss Skillane, Mrs Venn?'

'Indeed I have, sir. A fine young lady of the very best stamp.'

'We are going to Cornwall to rescue her.'

'As I am sure will please her greatly. Oh my Lord, if it won't make her little heart sing! What a lovely thing to want to do, I am certain.'

CHAPTER FIFTEEN

West Cornwall; a nest of beaten-down ferns in a hollow a mile or so below Botallack, a little after ten in the morning. Looking towards the land, the clouds tumbling over the ridge are a strange cinnamon brown. But out to sea, the horizon is empty of anything but the palest light, stretched, it seems, like linen on the line. The wind is steady but spiteful. Though he has been in the Duchy less than a full day, Murch has learned to call the gust that did for his hat (sending it over the cliff edge like a falling chimney pot) a light breeze.

Murch has a very straightforward, phlegmatic approach to the task in hand. The gentlemen—Mr Kennett and Mr Westland—like to turn over all the possibilities that might arise from the Cornish expedition, many of which they rehearsed on the train going down. Though they travelled with first-class tickets, they sat with Murch for long periods in the lesser accommodation, something his fellow passengers regarded with the greatest suspicion.

'The law, are you?' a solicitor's clerk bound for Exeter asked.

'What makes you say that, chummie?'

'I know the Old Bill when I see it. Detectives, is it?'

'Do you know anything about brass-rubbings? No? Well, that's what we're about. So smoke your pipe and read your book, you yellow-toothed old bugger.'

'Oh, very nice language, I must say,' the elderly clerk muttered. But resumed his study of *The*

178

Widow's Secret, by that master of the genre, Henry Ellis Margam.

Murch yawned and closed his eyes, arms folded across his chest. It would be too much to say that he slept but neither was he in the least exercised by what lay ahead. There was an element of vanity in this: while talk was all very well, he knew he was there to finish this cove Judd and if possible keep the other two out of mischief. He could have done with a weapon of some sort but kept a polite silence when schemes and stratagems were being discussed—if you like, he indulged the gentlemen. In Murch's experience, the only sure way to finish someone was to get close, square up to the cove and punch his ticket for him.

With or without a weapon, he looked forward to doing just that. He admired William Kennett for his reckless passion (and choice of housekeeper). Mr Westland, however, was in his opinion not quite the finished article. Murch, though a shy man himself, did not understand shyness in others and Westland's gentle hesitancy occasionally dismayed him. When the party finally left the train at St Erth and a discussion began about where to stay—or as Westland put it—where to hide themselves away, Murch hoisted his knapsack and said, if it was all the same to the gentlemen, he would sooner walk over to St Just that night and make his number with this Linny girl as quick as may be.

'But how will you know where to find the place?' Philip Westland asked, bewildered.

'I have a tongue in my head,' Murch responded, with just enough of a smile for it not to be a complete reproof. He touched the brim of his battered beaver and strode away. Kennett

179

attempted to call him back and got by way of reply a brief but emphatic wave goodbye.

'At ten tomorrow, then, at the girl's cottage,' Philip shouted. But this time there was not even a wave.

'What we were vain enough to call a plan in London looks very different down here,' Philip observed uneasily.

'Then how does it seem to you now?' asked Kennett.

'Like a recipe for disaster.'

A station porter ambled towards them with a note. It was from Bella, who was eight hours ahead of them and already installed at Boskeriss House. Philip read it with dismay.

'Where is Lelant?' he asked the porter.

'A fair step,' the man replied.

*   *   *

From his vantage in the ferns, Murch watched something he could not have bargained for in a month of Sundays: the replica of the *Mary Skillane* coming down the hill in a cart pulled by a fat-bellied grey horse. For a few magical stretches the horse and cart disappeared from view and then the ship seemed to buck and roll in a green Atlantic trough, stupendous mountain ranges to its lee. It sailed with bare poles (save for a whimsically hoisted jib), yet even so its detailed elegance sang like a seabird. The hull was painted a glossy black, decorated by a single line of darkest green. The deck was of varnished oak planking, the hatches in some darker wood. Every detail of the rigging and running lines was exact and to scale. The shrouds whistled and the halyards clattered just as they would if the *Mary Skillane* were really at sea. Murch was entranced.

Linny Trethewey lay on her back beside him, the baby asleep on her naked breast.

'You don't want to see any of this go by?' Murch asked.

'Wouldn't mind burning that old boat, tipping it out the cart and setting fire to it. And piss on the embers, I would.'

'Living up here has done you no favours. There's more than a ha'p'orth of patience has gone into that bit of carpentry.'

'You talk funny,' she said. 'The way you speak. And croaky like some old crow. And that silly hat! Baby likes you, though.'

Murch studied her much as if she were the baby's older and more slow-witted sister. 'Back to the cottage then,' he suggested.

'Cottage, you call it! That's what I mean. What do you live in, up there in London?'

'Button your blouse, Linny, and let's go make ourselves a pot of tea.'

Far from buttoning up, Linny ran a hand inside the dirty cotton and caressed herself luxuriously, with more than half an eye to the effect she was creating. This was a waste of her time: Murch's expression remained utterly neutral. She took him to be embarrassed.

'Would I like it in London?' she cooed from under lowered lashes.

'Not much,' he admitted with his usual honesty. 'But who's to say you must live there?'

'Well, you can keep bloody old Cornwall, I'll tell you that.'

181

'Don't tell me. Tell the two gentlemen who are coming to help you.'

'Yes, and where are they? I don't see 'un galloping to the rescue, same as you say they would. Don't see no purse of gold, same as you promised.'

Murch stood and pulled her up by her arms. 'Give me the child,' he said.

She was in the act of passing him across when a rifle shot rang out. The sound of it was like a dry crack, much amplified. Murch knew at once what it was, roughly where it came from, and from how far away. He threw himself on top of Linny and clawed the baby under his arm. The smell of fresh blood cut like a knife through the faintly sickly smell of crushed ferns.

'Be still,' he whispered. 'There won't be another so long as we don't stand up.'

'Am I dying?'

'Not for many a year yet. Lie still and bear the pain a moment longer. The baby's safe.'

Linny's eyelids fluttered and her eyes rolled back to the whites. Murch dragged back the fabric to her blouse. The blood was comfortingly bright red and ran down into her armpit in thin rivulets. He pulled his handkerchief from his neck and pressed it down on the puckered entry wound. The baby was bawling its head off. But that was what Murch supposed babies did, most of the time. He patted its stomach absent-mindedly.

'We have been sniped at,' he explained. 'But your ma's a big healthy girl and there's no need to take on. So give it a rest for five minutes, there's a good lad.'

'And then he spirited them both away,' Kennett concluded. 'The bullet passed clean through her. The child is uninjured.'

Bella's face as pale as paper. 'He did not take them both back to the cottage?'

'The pig sty,' Kennett corrected. 'Hellhole a better description still. Yes, they went back there and that is where we found his note. After we read it, we burned the place to the ground. Where they are now is anyone's guess.'

'You set fire to her only home?' Bella asked faintly.

'What Philip called forcing the pace. If you like, burning our boats behind us. If Judd was still there, still watching, that was the message it gave out, surely?'

They met by arrangement at an out-of-the-way inn along the road to Lelant Sands. It was a twenty-minute walk from Boskeriss House and to add plausibility to her absence Bella carried a stamped letter, addressed to Mrs Hannah Bardsoe of Shelton Street, but in reality a note to Kennett from Mary Skillane.

They had Mary's word for it that the inn was a safe rendezvous. Kennett and Westland had taken rooms there the previous night as London gentlemen with a taste for ornithology. Their mention of a hunt for the European fish eagle, which they hoped to accomplish on horseback, had caused convulsions of silent mirth when announced.

'Where is Philip now?' Bella demanded.

'Asking after the three of them along the road

from St Just to Newlyn. But it will not be so easy as that. Listen, Bella. It is certain that Judd is the villain that tried to kill that poor child. I have seen the ground and it was not a close-to shot. He tried to pick her off at range. She is a very lucky girl.'

'He was not attempting simply to warn her, or frighten her?'

'Murch says not.'

Bella bit her lip. At the landlord's suggestion they were drinking hot rum punch, though it was hardly past four in the afternoon. The room they sat in was empty, though they could hear a low murmur of voices from the public side of the house. A buffeting wind rattled the windows and to Bella's dismay it had begun to rain.

Kennett laid his hand over hers. 'It is bad,' he said. 'How are things up at Boskeriss House?'

'Lady Skillane is doing her best.'

'And?'

'I imagine the news you really want to hear is contained in Mary's letter.'

'I was thinking rather of Judd's latest movements,' he replied sharply.

Bella ducked her head in contrition. 'The comings and goings in that place are almost impossible to track. Some people arrived today whom I took to be butchers, or greengrocers. They were the Mayor of Camborne and his lady. There is a very corpulent gentleman in a black velvet suit who describes himself as Sir William's agent in Falmouth. In point of manners, this place is hardly out of the eighteenth century.'

'And Judd?'

'Has not been seen since yesterday. It is said he went by horseback last night to oversee the transport of this cursed ship model from St Just. It forms the centrepiece of the celebrations being got up for the new library.'

'So off he set with a rifle around his neck,' he muttered.

Bella flushed with anger. 'Around his neck or across the saddle of his horse. I did not see him leave,' she said brusquely.

She and Robert Judd had paid each other only perfunctory greetings since meeting and her time had been largely taken up in trying to keep warm in the most uncomfortable house of its size she had ever visited. Lady Skillane seemed to think that tea was the only lubricant to conversation, so much so that Bella felt herself to be followed about by rattling trays, often moving from one room of cups and dainty little cakes, only to be ambushed an hour later in another. And, much as she liked Mary Skillane, she was being dogged by her wherever she went. The only place she could be alone to think was in her bathroom. It was also where she smoked, wrapped in a blanket with nothing to look at but the lavatory bowl.

The evening meal was suitably aldermanic—an immense leg of lamb, some sort of ragout that might or might not have been rabbit, heaped with wild mushrooms and spiced sausages, lobsters, and a mighty turbot. The service was chaotic and the wines seemed to appear randomly at the whim of the butler. It was clearly a mark of respect to eat and drink prodigiously. The sound of cutlery upon plates made a din that almost defeated what conversation there was.

'You have paid us the honour of travelling a very long way to share our Cornish home, Mrs Wallis,'

185

Skillane boomed down the table.

'It is my first visit to the Duchy, Sir William,' Bella replied. 'I have much to learn.'

'Do you hear often of Cornwall in London?' the Mayor of Camborne's wife enquired.

'It is spoken of as the ancient nursery of seafaring,' Bella improvised. 'From Drake down, scratch a sailor, find a Cornishman.'

'That is well said,' Sir William laughed. 'Though I should tell you the most recent arrests for smuggling were made around the point in St Ives only a year or so since. Scratch a Cornishman, find a rogue.'

At which there was much cheerful banging of spoons and stamping of feet. Bella stole a glance at Judd. He was exploring his teeth with his tongue, as though too bored to be convivial. There were high spots of colour on his cheek. When the men joined the ladies for coffee after the meal, he was nowhere to be found.

Bella forced her mind back to Kennett and the here and now. The little wainscotted room they sat in stank of tobacco and woodsmoke and was decorated by a single framed print, a steel engraving of the 'Queen Visiting her Poorer Neighbours'. This great event had clearly taken place at Balmoral and Her Majesty, dressed in widow's weeds, was shown forcing an improving text on to a bewildered old couple at their cottage door. Two of her daughters watched unsmilingly.

For something to do, Bella rose and straightened this picture, her hands trembling on the frame. 'The weekend proper begins tomorrow with a semi-public dinner at which forty will sit down,' she said none too steadily. 'It is

186

inconceivable that Judd should be absent from that. There will be toasts and speeches from Skillane's hangers-on and Lady Skillane has arranged for telegrams to be sent from what she calls more distant parts. We must have that girl safely under our hand long before then.' She turned back to Kennett with a downturned mouth. 'Something you planned to achieve this morning, of course.'

'We were late because we were lost,' he replied tetchily. 'We were lost because we had not a decent map between us. Westland on horseback is like watching Gladstone attempt to play polo. As for signposts, they are as rare in Cornwall as hens' teeth.'

'Well, we must find Murch and his party before the sun goes down today.'

'You are fractious, Bella,' Kennett said in a low voice.

'Oh, do you think so? I wonder how that can be.'

'And now you are waspish.'

'I am virtually a prisoner to circumstance, huddled up in Skillane's house with people I detest,' she exclaimed. 'I depend entirely upon you and Philip to effect our plan, such as it is, and yes, I am fractious. I will go further. I am very close to being distraught.'

'I hope Mary is some sort of comfort to you.'

She wanted to tell him that much as she loved Mary Skillane, her foot itched to kick her on the shins for the inexhaustible solicitudes she offered. But just at that point the door banged open and Philip Westland walked in, covered in mud from head to foot, the landlord hard on his heels with a kettle of rum punch.

'If God intended me to be a horseman, he should have given my parents an earlier indication of His wishes and desires,' Philip complained. 'I have been in company with—I cannot say I have ridden—an obstreperous mare called Sugar. The most misleading name in all ostlery. So soon as she sensed we were going home and not beating about the bush like fools, she came back at a gallop. Sometimes with me in the saddle and sometimes not.'

'Ah well,' the landlord commented, trying hard to keep a straight face. 'The old fish eagle is a flighty sort and hard to find in these parts. But see thee now, sir, do you have some of this here punch, that is hot and hot and will restore your good nature. As for Sugar, I shall speak to her, you have my word on it. Can be right moody when she's minded and only a master horseman could have brought her home so tidy.'

'You are not laughing up your sleeve at me at all, landlord?'

'Never in life, sir.'

After he had left and Philip had dragged off his topcoat, he bent to kiss Bella on her brow. And then, briefly, her lips.

'They are safe,' he said in a low voice. 'Murch has them at an inn outside Newbridge and an arrangement has been made to bring them by covered cart to Penzance later today. She has been seen by a doctor and the baby is well. Our friend has performed wonders.'

'What is there in Penzance?'

'They will stay in Penalverne Drive, next door to the police station. According to Murch, the landlady of that place is a widow from

188

Bermondsey, which he considers an advantage. More to the point, her late husband was a sergeant of the West Kents. In Murch's eyes there can be no higher commendation.'

'We seem to know a great deal about these lodgings.'

'Widow Harvey and the landlady of the inn at Newbridge are sisters.'

Bella considered, while watching Philip pull off his boots like any squire and extend his stockinged feet to the fire.

'We have the girl safe? You can be categorical about that?' she asked. Philip winced but managed not to shout out loud in exasperation. Bella rose and kissed him guiltily on the cheek. 'Poor Philip. I apologise. Kennett will tell you, I am fit to throw away,' she said.

'We have done as much we can, Bella. Better you tell us what you have planned for tomorrow.'

'At this dinner, or banquet as Lady Skillane is apt to describe it, there should be a telegram of congratulation from Linny Trethewey and her child,' she suggested. 'And, if it doesn't sound too ghoulish, one from Mrs Liza Givens and, if Murch will wear it, Molly Clunn. I will offer to explain them all for the benefit of otherwise mystified guests.'

Kennett looked up. 'You mean to unmask Judd there and then? In front of forty people?'

'I cannot think of a better moment.'

'Nor a safer one,' Philip added thoughtfully.

'I don't like it,' Kennett decided. 'It would lead to the table being thrown into an uproar at any address in London to be sure, but may not hit the mark in this benighted wilderness.'

'I think we are doing all this to open Skillane's eyes and save Mary from Judd's clutches,' Philip said gently. 'I would have thought it will at least accomplish that.'

'And all the rest? Murder, attempted murder?' Kennett asked.

'Will fall out, choosing its own time.'

'As it might be the fox turning and trotting back towards the huntsmen, the better to oblige them. Is that your plan?'

'Do you have a better?'

'We need Linny to appear in person,' Kennett said.

'That is asking too much of her.' These words were spoken by a newcomer, a rain-soaked figure standing in the crooked doorway. His sudden entry had the effect of rendering them all speechless. It was of course Robert Judd. He nodded to Bella, pushed Kennett out of the way, sat down against the fire, and, like Westland, opened his coat.

'I very kindly volunteered to come and collect you, Mrs Wallis. The tide is on the turn and has brought in rain. I have the chaise outside and will take you home in it. Sir William is anxious you should not catch cold.'

'You have the cheek of the devil,' Bella said in a wondering tone. 'How did you know where to find me?'

Judd's smile turned into a laugh. 'Do you suppose it was so very difficult? Throw a handful of silver into the mud here and any of a dozen poor devils will scrabble to do your bidding.'

'You put it with your usual elegance, Mr Judd.'

'You don't like the picture I draw? What else is this but a story about money?' he continued in the most conversational tone possible. 'More money than you can begin to imagine. I don't think you have fully understood that yet, my dear Mrs Wallis. But that is how we must settle the question.'

'The question is about murder and attempted murder,' Bella rejoined. 'Blackmail and extortion. The ruination of a simple country girl who, for all you care, is bleeding to death out at Botallack this very minute.'

'These are relatively unimportant matters.'

'Are you quite mad?' Kennett shouted, his whole body trembling.

Judd merely waved the question away. His effrontery was breathtaking. When the landlord poked his head around the door, Judd ordered a brandy with the greatest nonchalance and then turned back to Bella. 'With a little ingenuity we can work things out to our mutual advantage,' he continued, his eyes fixed only on her. 'You and your friends have a shared mission in life—to interfere in matters which don't concern you. I'll pay you the courtesy of supposing you came here with a plan of action. It hasn't worked. How could it? I am the sort of man you cannot begin to understand or master.'

'We have the girl,' Bella said.

'And I have one of my own, Mrs Wallis. The sweet and virginal Miss Skillane.'

'You will leave her alone!' Kennett roared.

Judd pointed his finger at him. 'On the contrary. Unless you agree to see things my way, I will debauch that poor creature tonight in such fashion she will never entertain another man again. Mere rape won't come into it.'

'You unutterable swine!'

191

'Just so. Did you think to threaten me with Linny Trethewey? You poor fool, Kennett. I will send that girl of yours into an asylum for you.' The pistol that appeared as if by magic in his hand was very real. Even under the guise of a playful gesture, the weapon's muzzle was pointed directly at Bella's chest. 'Before you, Mr Westland, or you, Mr Kennett, contemplate anything foolish, I must warn you I will blow a hole in Mrs Wallis you can put your fist in. I will not hesitate.'

'And then you'll swing for it,' Bella said, surprising herself at the steadiness of her voice.

'Maybe. But this is a part of the country steeped in the idea of false witness. Put another way, money talks here. Some foolish horseplay with a loaded pistol, Mr Kennett maddened with desire, Mr Westland trying to remember exactly what day it was. All the parties dead drunk on rum punch. And the delightful Mrs Wallis there on the floor, dead as a door knocker.'

'You place a great deal of faith in the power of money,' Philip observed.

'Would you care to put it to the test?'

Kennett broke free from Philip's restraining grasp and with an inhuman howl threw himself at their tormentor. For a part of a second Bella felt her skin crawl, expecting Judd to keep his promise. Instead, the pistol came up and smashed Kennett in the mouth. He fell against a chair and sprawled face-up on the floor. Judd was on him like a flash, the muzzle pushed against one eye.

'You shall be the first to understand,' he whispered. 'You know who I am and what I am capable of.'

Later, months later, Bella would wonder why

192

she and Philip Westland did not rush him then and there; or, less romantically, why she did not fling herself out of the door and run to the protection of the public bar. The answer was in Judd's next remark.

'I am teaching you all something valuable—that a really determined man will do anything if the stakes are high enough.'

'Let him up,' Westland said.

And Judd did scramble off Kennett's chest, brushing the sweat from his face with the hand that held the pistol. For the sheer crudity of doing it, he spat into the fire. His eyes were dark as coals. 'I see by the agitation of your breath you begin to understand, Mrs Wallis. So. This is how it will be. You will return with me to the great house and enjoy Sir William's generous hospitality. The gentlemen will settle their bill here and when they are safely on the morning train to London, things will return to how I wish them to be.'

'Put up your gun now, Mr Judd,' Bella said. 'That, or shoot me. But you are not going to do that, are you? That would hardly advance your immediate plans.'

Judd looked at her with something approaching respect. 'I think not. Or at any rate, not until we have agreed how things must be.'

'They can be however you want them. But the landlord will be back in a moment. For your own sake, put up the gun.'

He hesitated a moment, and then laid the pistol in his lap. 'You are worth two of any man of your acquaintance, Mrs Wallis. However. Kennett believes me. And now, I think, so do you.'

'That you are contemptible beyond words? I

have always thought so.'

'You need not say any more, Bella,' Philip warned in his gentlest voice.

Judd laughed. 'The excellent Mr Westland! A little late in protecting the honour of his lady but then he has the outlook of a gentleman. The world as seen from clubhouse windows in Jermyn Street. Well, I spit on all that. I spit on you, all of you.'

He perked up his pistol in warning as Westland rose, but the big man simply shrugged, and with a half-smile, dug into his greatcoat pockets for his cheroots. 'You have us beat, Judd,' he said, amiably enough. 'And I suppose I must congratulate you for playing a weak hand with consummate skill.'

'Is it really such a weak hand?' Judd asked. 'Do as I say and by Monday next, you will have Mrs Wallis returned to you unharmed. Kennett will have his simpering ninny arranging the water-colours at the house in Chiswick—and not trying to wash herself clean of horrors and nightmares she cannot name. The clocks will still run forward, you will all have had a mild adventure, with the certainty that you will never see me again. As for the rest of it, none of which concerns you, you may read about it in the papers in due course.'

'You think that is who we are?' Bella asked.

Judd flicked the pistol at Bella one last time. 'I know so. You are children when it comes to this game. Go back to your drawing-room tittle-tattle, Mrs Wallis. Buy a new dress. Read some diverting novel, maybe.'

'Your arrogance will win you prizes in any country in the world, Mr Judd.'

For a second or so, she saw something pass

194

across his face she had not bargained for.

'You think that's what this is? You talk to me about arrogance? I am out of a box you should never have opened. What you are looking at, Mrs Wallis, is evil. You are not equipped to deal with it. Now, if you are ready, we shall leave.'

'Don't go back to the house with him, Bella,' Kennett mumbled through bloody teeth.

'I have to go,' she replied. She moved to Philip and kissed him on the lips. 'He has thought of everything. Or almost everything.'

It was a poorly coded remark that Judd destroyed with his most brutal laugh. 'You are referring to your man Murch, I don't doubt. He is dead—or if not yet, he will be before sunset.'

Though she felt as far from laughter as Cornwall was from Timbuktu, this promise from Judd brought out a broad smile. There were tears in her eyes to be sure; but with them came the sudden flash of something almost approaching a grin.

'You think as I have seen you eat, Mr Judd. I would back Billy Murch against you or any dozen of your hired cut-throats. As you will soon enough discover. My cape, if you please.'

'Fetch your own cape.'

'Do as I say, you ridiculous creature.'

Judd hesitated; and then threw the cape across the parlour. Bella caught it, smiling. 'And now fetch the chaise round to the door.'

CHAPTER SIXTEEN

That evening at Boskeriss House, the usual clatter of determined eating was drowned by the gunshot staccato of mallets, as elsewhere in the house the carpenters hired by Sir William assembled the pre-cut sections of the library loft. Sir William himself was supervising the work and the loudest of the imprecations coming from this distant uproar were his.

Accordingly, the duties of host fell to Judd, who sprawled silent, offhand and, to all outward appearances, drunk. Bella watched him carefully, nevertheless. Although she had won a small skirmish at the inn, the battle was still going his way. She was, as she had told William Kennett, completely a victim of circumstance while in the house. And Boskeriss House *en fête* was a little like a Hogarthian print or an opera by John Gay. The Skillane guests had a very simple view of dinner parties: they were a chance to rampage. Bella discovered the truth of an old cliché: she simply could not hear herself think.

For example, to paper over the cracks that were appearing, the Mayor of Camborne took it upon himself to entertain the company with a stream of anecdotes about the character of the God-bothered Cornish peasantry. The comic dialect he employed came not from an actor's repertoire but was his natural habit of speech, one that he had only smothered in recent years. His wife had the grace to look anguished. For her part, Lady Skillane looked as though she would like nothing more than to crawl across the table and hide in the trifle. Her daughter sat with silent tears coursing down her cheeks and collecting in little candlelit diamonds along her jawline.

Bella's dinner partner was a pleasant enough old man called Coombes, who hardly needed to mention that he had lost his wife some four years since, so gently abject was his address. The first part of the meal had been taken up with his monologue touching the mystery of the five red balls that decorated the Duchy's scutcheon: Bella had nothing to contribute to the subject. Coombes tried again with questions about the character of Mr Gladstone and (more impertinently) the Princess of Wales. There was no real harm in this—for Mr Coombes, London was as remote and unintelligible as St Petersburg. He had never been to either place. Some common ground could be had from a discussion about whether fish had feelings. The old Cornishman felt they must— trout and salmon certainly, but even (he dared assert) pilchards. And all this while came an infernal racket from the library.

'I know carpentry, Mrs Wallis,' he said, making one last effort, 'and that loft of Sir William's is a very clever piece of design. All the drawings are his, you understand, and there's a man—'

'There's a man could steal pennies from a beggar's cup,' Judd supplied, to the consternation of those who heard him.

'If there's a finer gentleman to come out of Cornwall I should like to meet him,' Coombes quavered, at first defiant and then, when he caught Judd's ironic glance, blushing crimson.

'You know our host well, sir?' Bella suggested.

197

'I am his banker, madam,' he mumbled. 'Which honour I have had for twenty years or more.'

'And do you stay here tonight as his guest?'

'Tonight I sleep at home. Which is over to Crippleasease.'

Bella looked very meaningfully into his innocent blue eyes. 'And does your way lie by Lelant at all?' she murmured—but not low enough to escape Judd's rancorous attention.

'It does not,' he shouted from the top of the table. 'Beware, Coombes, you are in danger of being propositioned by a beautiful London widow.'

The old man flushed. Bella was astonished to feel his bony hand land suddenly high up upon her thigh, not lightly either, but with a firm pressure. She turned her head away from Judd so that he could not see her lips.

'I ask because I need your help,' she said.

'What are you telling him now, Mrs Wallis?' Judd demanded.

'That you appear to be drunk, sir,' Bella replied, careless of the reaction she got from an agonised Lady Skillane.

The old man's grip tightened on her for a moment, enough to stiffen her back. She began to wonder whether he had misunderstood the moment.

But then Coombes smiled and patted her leg gently before resuming his knife and fork. 'I go by back roads to Crippleasease,' he explained. Then he added something else cautious and for her ears only. 'In the normal course of things, Lelant is quite out of my way.'

But even this whisper reached the top of the table where Judd was watching them, his eyes glistening. 'Be sure you make it so tonight,' he bellowed, truculent.

After pudding and the usual confusion with cheese and fruit, it was considered a happy suggestion for the dinner guests to inspect the library. Bella excused herself for a moment and ran upstairs. Nor was there anything very suspicious in this—it seemed that in Cornwall people liked to get up from table and wander about helplessly, sometimes taking coffee, sometimes staggering out into the fresh air, like guests at a wedding.

The significance of the work taking place was well understood. The finale to the following night's banquet was to be the ceremonial hoisting of the *Mary Skillane* to its place of honour. There was already competition among Sir William's closer cronies to lend a hand to see it triumphantly home. The man appointed to oversee this work was the bosun of the St Ives lifeboat. When Bella came down from her room, Coombes was nowhere to be seen but Bosun Priddy stood with his hands on his hips, shaking his head in a very mannered way. Bella exchanged a few words with him.

'Ais, missus,' the man said, sucking his teeth gloomily, 'they heroes on the tally ropes tomorrow had better not be took by drink. For there's no more than an inch of clearance between the mainmast of the *Mary* and that there ceiling. And bugger all use will she be to anybody if she sits up there broached like some old Cardiff coal brig.'

'Have you sailed with Sir William ever, Mr Priddy?'

'I have not,' Priddy replied emphatically. 'I was—I am—an Edward Hain man. Not the boy,

199

mind you: his father.'

'There is a boy?'

'A man in years. But a pen-pusher, a desk man. No, I speak of the father now. In the year '62 we took his old brigantine, the *Emily*, a fifteen-month voyage, as far as Brazil and up the seaboard all the way to Canada. Now there's a hero for you. Mr Hain would not take a morsel of food from this fellow's table, no, not if it was the last on God's earth. I speak frankly.'

'A different kind of gentleman?' Bella suggested.

'Why,' Priddy cried, 'there have been seagoing Hains here nigh on four centuries. This upstart bugger come out of a potato field. And don't it show?'

Bella realised tardily that though he wished sobriety on others, Bosun Priddy was himself catastrophically drunk.

'I am astonished you have agreed to help Sir William at all.'

'Ah, but when she struck that day at Porthloe, the *Mary*, fourteen souls were lost. One of them the wife's brother, a child, an unshaved boy. And where is he buried? Nowhere! How and for why? Because his body was never recovered. Him and two others. Never seen again.'

'And that's why you took the job?'

'Eh?' Priddy asked, momentarily confused. 'No, no. It was this. It is only ever this.'

He rubbed his thumb against his forefinger, managing to look sly and guilty all at the same time. Then knuckled his forehead and ambled away.

Bella turned and found Coombes at her elbow, already in his old-fashioned topcoat, buttoned to the neck. On his head was a ridiculous sealskin cap, the flaps sticking out at right angles.

'Be quick,' he whispered.

*   *   *

'My mother is at her wits' end,' Mary confided dolefully an hour later in Bella's bedroom. 'She is not particularly worldly, as you have seen. But if I try to talk to her she buries her head in yet another list. Will there be enough proper serving spoons for tomorrow? Have we made sufficient arrangements for the coachmen and other servants? Above all, what if the accursed library is not finished?'

'Listen to me now, Mary,' Bella interrupted. 'I should like it if you stayed with me tonight. Go back to your bedroom, fetch your nightgown and then lock your door from the outside. Come straight back here.'

'What is happening?' the girl asked, bewildered.

'You are in mortal danger. And so am I.'

Not strictly true; not in mortal danger, she amended silently. Or at any rate, not yet.

*   *   *

Mr Coombes was an honourable man after his fashion, but he was, when all was said and done, a banker. He was (he reminded himself) obliged to Sir William above all others, a man who might have gone to Bolitho's with his business but had instead revived—plucked from disaster—a tiny bank that dealt with the petty people of that part of Cornwall. Sir William had made Coombes,

201

snatched him from obscurity and brought him clients he might never have met otherwise. These reflections were made all the keener for the driving rain that filled up his eyes on the road up to Cripplesease. There was only one house worthy of any attention in that village and he was going home to it. Was that to be counted as nothing?

It was in his nature to act prudently, as does any man who is born to be afraid of the world and its doings. Balance sheets were Coombes's refuge, silent regiments of figures that he might command without fear of defeat. Yet now he had just been at a calamitous dinner, sitting next to a beautiful woman whose scent still filled his nostrils, charged by her to deliver a letter to persons unknown at an inn of which he had never heard. There was giddiness in that it was better not to contemplate. For this reason he turned off along the road to Lelant and headed home.

'You are fifty-eight years old,' he scolded himself, thinking of Bella's warm thigh and—by vague association—her comely bust and wonderful grey eyes. Because he was that kind of man, he felt the presence of his late wife in the chaise beside him and seemed to hear, above the hissing of the wheels, her habitual dry laugh.

When the horse stopped stone-dead, he was very nearly pitched out of his seat into the muddy lane. He peered into the dark and thought he saw a fallen bough. When it reared up on end, Mr Coombes screamed and Jupiter, the horse, shied as if it would much prefer to go back the way they had come.

'Who is there?' Coombes yelped.

Murch's effort to stand proved too much for him

202

and he sat down again in a heaving splash. 'Are you going to help me or not, you bloody peasant?' he roared before falling once again on to his back.

*   *   *

Murch had been set upon by footpads or something of the sort. Not so much as a wet stick to defend himself, so took off across the moor, making a stand at a small quarry. Dished the young bloke with a handy rock to the head, fought a lengthy and seemingly inconclusive battle with the other cove; got him down at last with an abandoned shovel and near enough took his arm off at the elbow with it. For good measure, smacked him with the back of the blade, breaking his nose. Ran on. Felt a bit iffy. Found the road to Cripplesease, sat down for a rest. Keeled over.

The history of this adventure was written on his naked body. He lay on Mr Coombes's kitchen table with a bruise the size of a hen's egg at his temple, a flap of flesh where his right eyebrow should be, two broken ribs and a gash in his thigh as wide as a torn coat seam.

'And if you are not lucky to be alive,' Coombes's housekeeper said wonderingly.

'A few knocks and scratches,' Murch mumbled. 'The young one was neither use nor ornament but the other bloke knew what he was about.'

'Yes, and after you bested him, why did you bash him with that old shovel, break his nose and all?'

'To recognise him. We shall need to speak again tomorrow.'

The housekeeper nodded. She liked the way he submitted to her proddings and palpings, as though to be naked before a great fat woman like herself was nothing very special. She liked it too when he gasped and seized her hand as she set about stitching the gash in his leg. 'You are a rare plucked one,' she smiled, admiring the rise and fall of his surprisingly muscled stomach.

Coombes came into the room with a very large brandy. Murch indicated that his nurse should take the first sip. 'You understand,' he said to the master of the house, 'I have no idea where I am but I must set off again for Lelant quicker than jack spit.'

'Not while I finished this here embroidery,' the fat old housekeeper chuckled.

'To Lelant. Now why is that?' Coombes said with an awful foreboding.

'I have business with two gentlemen there.'

'Oh dear,' Mr Coombes muttered, fishing Bella's letter from his pocket. 'Oh dear, oh dear.'

Murch sat up with a racking groan, winced his way through a couple of breaths and held his hand out for the crumpled envelope. When Coombes hesitated, Murch shook his head to clear it, sending a little rain of grey sweat to the kitchen table.

'Be a gentleman now, sir,' he muttered. 'Unless I am mistook, this here note was given you tonight by what we might call the lady in the tower.'

'The lady—?'

'By Mrs Wallis,' Murch said, much more bluntly.

He fell back, exhausted. The housekeeper wiped the sweat from his brow.

Coombes passed across the envelope. 'Perhaps in a while a little of the chicken broth, Mrs Jeavons,' he suggested to his housekeeper, seeming to notice for the first time that they were standing over a stark naked man stretched out on the kitchen table, five candles at his head and feet, a bloody pudding cloth wedged against his thigh.

Murch was reading. When he had finished, he crumpled the note in his fist. 'Now we shall learn the full measure of your kindness,' he managed, before fainting.

*   *   *

'Which has been considerable,' Philip Westland told Coombes, pumping the old man's hand for the third time. He and Kennett paced about the old-fashioned sitting room, watched by two portraits that were of Coombes's ancestors and two more that might have been anybody. One wall was taken up entirely by a clumsy landscape tapestry, in which gentlemen on horseback leaped ditches and round-shouldered milkmaids huddled together in mob-caps. Dogs slunk around in the foreground, observed (perhaps commanded) by a parson in a tricorne hat, sporting a duck gun.

'To send your carriage to fetch us, that was handsomely done.'

'The thing is, I have no clear idea of what is happening,' Coombes said pitifully.

'There is mischief, great mischief,' Philip replied. 'Our friend Mrs Wallis is in the greatest danger from a man called Judd. I am sure you know the gentleman.'

'You do not make me any more easy in my mind,' the old man cried. 'I know Mr Judd to be a double-dyed villain.'

'Then you have some idea of our purpose,'

Kennett said.

Coombes looked very uncomfortably from one to the other. 'And the half-dead fellow I found in the roadway?'

'Is of our party. We shall need to speak to him.'

Murch was in Mrs Jeavons's double bed, while that good woman sat with a candle at her side, hands folded on the bible in her lap.

'He has took a terrible beating, gentlemen,' she whispered.

'Now, ma,' Murch replied from under a huge mound of blankets, 'I am just taking a little rest here and regrouping my forces, so to speak.'

'Is anything broken?' Philip asked.

'Ribs,' came the reply. 'So, nothing serious. If you or Mr Kennett can find me my trousers, perhaps Mrs Jeavons could run us up a pot of coffee.'

'At this hour of the morning!' she shrilled. 'You'll never sleep, you great daft man.'

'Something to think about,' Murch agreed drily.

He insisted on dressing and coming downstairs, one tread at a time, his face running with sweat. He hobbled to a chair in the kitchen, fussed over by Philip Westland. Mr Coombes came in, took one look and excused himself to bed.

'Whatever need you have of me, I am at your disposition, gentlemen, but I shall be much improved for an hour or so of dark and silence. I am not used to such excitement.'

'There is nothing to be done until first light, sir,' Murch wheezed, grasping his hand briefly.

'You have been through the mill, Billy,' Kennett muttered when Coombes had gone.

'I see you have something of a fat lip and busted

cheek yourself. If you gentlemen will tell me how we stand at present with that ugly bastard Judd, we can perhaps decide how to go on. Did you happen to notice whether the old gentleman who owns this place has any guns at all?'

'No,' Westland said, tightly. 'And we don't go down that road. We must get Bella and Miss Skillane out of Boskeriss House and on the first train to London. Indeed, anywhere out of Cornwall. If you like, we retreat. Taking our wounded with us.'

'That don't sit well with me, not at all.'

'Whether it does or not, that is what I have decided.'

Murch's smile was vague enough to be a flat contradiction of Philip's remark and its tone. He took his mug of coffee from Mrs Jeavons and patted her amiably on the rump. 'You'd know if your master has a gun or two in the house, ma,' he murmured. 'Because I do not like to leave a thing unfinished. The gentlemen and their lady friends should by all means be got on to the London train. When they are out of harm's way, they should telegraph for the Trethewey girl to follow. But I stay.'

'You'll do as I say,' Philip snapped.

Murch looked him over with an unsettling calmness. 'Why, Mr Westland, I do believe you forget yourself,' he said in a very even tone indeed. 'I am not your dog.'

'Lor' lummocks,' Mrs Jeavons interposed hastily, 'I see the fever is beginning to talk in you, Murch. To speak that way to a gentleman! We don't have them manners down here, wouldn't last long if we had. As far as I can follow it, the job is to

207

get the two ladies out of Boskeriss House and off to London. Does it have to be done surreptitious?'

'They will not be let go willingly,' Philip said.

'Why then, I do believe I am in the road to help you. For hasn't Mrs Ferris called on my help in the kitchens for this here banquet that has been spoke of for nigh on a fortnight?'

'Mrs Ferris?'

'Lady Skillane's cook, the ignorant old cow. I am called to be there at eight but I reckon I'll find her at six, running about with her pinny over her head. In I shall go with the fishermen and their lobsters—for they are to have lobsters cooked in champagne tonight if you please—and it will be my pleasure to find your ladies and lay out what is to be done.'

'Brilliant!' Kennett exclaimed. 'And if we then are in the drive—'

'There is still a great risk to you, Mrs Jeavons,' Philip warned in a slow doubtful way.

'From Mr Judd, do you mean? I ain't afeared of him, nonewise. I heard you speak of Linny Trethewey a moment back and I will tell you straight there isn't a Christian soul for miles around that doesn't know that sad story. Any man who is against Judd—which is to say most local men—will keep me safe. And more than that, I flatter myself my wits ain't completely deserted me, fat old whale as I may be.'

'Who says you're a fat old whale?' Murch laughed. 'Bring me that cove and I will lay him out like a rolled carpet.'

'Oh, you can leave this one behind!' Mrs Jeavons cried, delighted. 'I'll show him a bit of Cornwall he won't forget in a hurry.'

'What do you say, Billy? Can it be done?'

'Anything can be done, Mr Westland. If that's how you want to end it, then nothing could be simpler. Nor wiser. It is no place for a lady, that I grant.'

'And you'll come with us?'

'In a day or two, for sure. When the dust down here has settled.'

Westland looked at him with very uneasy feelings. To call what he had proposed a retreat was merely a more dignified way of describing running away—and not just from Cornwall either. What he wanted was an end to the whole story, like slamming shut the pages of a book. In this light, Billy Murch's battered countenance was a fairly obvious reproach.

'You have done what you could, Mr Westland, and come as far as any man in London would wish to go. Things will look very different by dinnertime tonight, when you are back safe in the smoke.'

'Have you ever been told you are a stubborn and awkward terrier of a man, Mr Murch?'

'Not in those exact words. But stubborn has come into it from time to time. Yes.'

Or remorseless, Philip thought. 'I don't want any more trouble,' he warned.

At which even Kennett laughed.

CHAPTER SEVENTEEN

Bella lay in bed half awake, Mary Skillane's arm flung across her neck. The two had talked and argued until past two in the morning. The older woman had discovered something about the elfin Mary that would one day tax William Kennett in ways he could not have foreseen. The light of his life snored. Gently, to be sure, but once in a while with a great shuddering sob that would wake a dead man. This would be followed by a lengthy brrrf! and what could only be described as random champing.

In every other respect, Mary Skillane was a perfect bedfellow, slim, chaste, and warm as toast. Having made up her mind about running away from her parents on probably the worst day possible for them, she fell asleep almost at once, her head in the crook of Bella's neck. And as for the physical contact that happens when two people share the same bed, she was joyfully unselfconscious of it. With only the very faintest tinge of envy, Bella judged that if Kennett could set aside the snoring, his future happiness lay before him like a field of poppies.

At six thirty exactly there was a gentle tapping on the door. Bella stiffened. She had only one weapon to hand, a silver candlestick, and with that she jumped out of bed and laid her ear to the door. 'Who is it?' she whispered.

'A friend,' a woman's voice whispered back. 'Open the door and let me in, for all love.'

It was Mrs Jeavons, in kitchen pinafore and mob-cap. She made a bob to Bella and grasped the lady's hands in hers, explaining who she was and where she came from, mentioning that the house was still asleep, save for the servants, and that two gentlemen were waiting outside in the rain, each with his own gig. 'And nothing will do now but that you dress as double-quick as can be and join them, for if there is danger in the plan it is that old Judd will throw up his windows and spy those same two sportsmen, what have come to spirit you away to London. And then who knows what?'

'Their names?' Bella demanded.

'Kennett and Westland. Oh, 'tis all quite as it should be. The password is Fleur de Lys.'

'We were otherwise planning on making a rope from sheets and shinnying down the outside wall,' Bella explained hazily.

'Stairs is more practical,' Mrs Jeavons said. 'Now wake up that young missy and let's be off. I have put up sangwidges for you to break your fast and they say there is something more substantial to be had on the train itself. And if this isn't today's most romantic thing to happen in all Cornwall, then I don't know what is.'

The fat old Cornishwoman busied herself with waking and dressing Mary Skillane. Perhaps without all the rush and whispered urgings the girl might have changed her mind about leaving. 'But I can't go to London dressed in an evening gown,' she protested feebly.

'And far better you be flustered about such small things, rather than the earthquake you will leave behind,' Mrs Jeavons chided briskly. Mary at once burst into tears.

Bella cupped the girl's chin in her hands. 'This is a very big thing that you do, I realise. But you are doing it for a man who loves you. In time your parents will see it in the proper light. Your father has been most cruelly blackmailed into offering you to Judd and in the next two minutes both of you will be free of at least one disastrous consequence of that evil man's schemings.'

211

'Very well put, but enough said, my dear,' Mrs Jeavons interrupted. 'Now let us run down them old marble stairs like squirrels out of a tree.'

Though the house was as quiet as promised, the front door opened on to a very unwelcome scene. Standing on the gravel of the drive, dressed as for morning bathing, was Sir William Skillane. Unshaved, his white hair in wild disorder, the Guernsey sweater hanging from his shoulders in ruined swags, the master of Boskeriss swung his head this way and that from Philip Westland to William Kennett. He was trying to work out without being told what two carriages were doing drawn up in front of his house at that time of the morning.

Philip Westland raised his hat but could find nothing to say. Skillane narrowed his eyes. He glanced back to the house and saw Bella and his daughter on the threshold, as nervy as deer. He looked back and studied Kennett. 'You are the certain gentleman friend of my daughter's from London?'

'Yes,' Kennett croaked.

Skillane went over it all again, glancing from the carriages to the women in the doorway and back again. Absent-mindedly, he fondled the muzzle of one of the horses.

'You must know that your house and family and your fortune are in the gravest danger from Mr Robert Judd and his schemes,' Philip stated defiantly by way of helping him make up his mind.

Skillane looked up sharply. Some of the steel with which he had made his fortune—and kept it—seemed to reappear in his expression. 'You dare to presume what I should and should not know? And you tell me this on my own property?'

'I am explaining why we are here.'

'My daughter has invited you?'

'Sir William, you know very well you can command your daughter with a single word and she will stay. But I think you are wiser and perhaps nobler than that.'

When Kennett opened his mouth to add remarks of his own, Philip silenced him with a sharp gesture. There was a jingle of harness and the ugly screech of gulls over the roof of the house, but otherwise no human sound.

Skillane stood as still as a statue. 'Mary, come down from those steps, please,' he called at last.

In that instant, when the girl flew sobbing to her father, Bella thought they had lost the argument and William Kennett the love of his life. But Skillane surprised them all. Holding his daughter at arm's length, he looked into her eyes for a long second or two, embraced her—and then, without another word, tramped off down towards the beach.

'We may go,' Philip Westland said in his smallest voice, beckoning to Bella. Kennett reached down and helped Mary into the chaise. The horses were woken up to their duty and the chaises began to roll. Once on the road a canter through the rain became a gallop, the carriage wheels scattering clumpy spews of sand. There was nobody about save a few men on the beach.

Out in the bay, a schooner-rigged vessel came up head to wind in a creamy curve and let all canvas go. It was, Bella considered, a fitting punctuation and the end to the Cornwall adventure. From the moment Skillane had let his daughter go, the curtain had begun to come down on the whole drama. She trusted to Henry Ellis Margam to transform this mad dash along the road to St Erth into something more poetical—the midnight flight from a Bohemian castle, or a frantic lunge to safety across the Mont St Michel causeway.

'How clever you are,' she shouted to Philip Westland meanwhile.

'It is the horse you should be talking to,' he shouted back. 'Because I am hanged if I know how to steer or stop.'

It was unromantic, but that in itself was deeply satisfying to Bella. Buffeted about by the action of the chaise's springs, her arms around the waist of the man she loved, who gave a damn about Margam and the world of sensationalist fiction. The pins to her hair were down, her arms and breast were blue with cold and she would have given a year's income for a cup of coffee.

Somewhere up ahead there was the sheer ordinariness of a two-platform railway station and the dusty comforts of a first-class carriage. After that, the mild terrors of the Tamar gorge, over which the trains seemed to tiptoe and the boats below looked no larger than toys. And after that, pleasantly empty hours leading at last to the calm and elegance of the house in Orange Street. It was not the perfect outcome to such an almighty confusion of hate and greed, but nevertheless that was how Bella thought it should end.

In the train, she snatched a glance at her companions. Mary Skillane was asleep on Kennett's shoulder, her one visible hand screwed into a tiny fist, like a baby's. As for Philip, he sat looking steadfastly out of the window, *The Times* across his knees. He sat with his back to the engine, so that he was studying the landscape as it passed and not as it came towards him. And this, she thought, is how we all must travel, with our backs to the future. How could it be worthwhile to try to read its dizzying, headlong rush? She moved her seat to join him and—after a moment or two—sought his hand.

*   *   *

In all his years of marriage Mr Coombes had never seen his wife naked and his knowledge of how his own sex looked was confined to the wardrobe mirror and one or two thrilling glimpses of a boy called Albert Triggs from the days of his childhood. Now, in the space of twelve hours, he had inspected at close range two grown men. One of them was Billy Murch and the other was the giant standing in his kitchen at that moment holding up his shirt.

'That was one bloody lucky miss, you bet,' Kashvili said, prodding the inside of his hairy thigh. 'I give Mr Kennett a thousand pounds, he can't make the same hole in me, not if he practise a year.'

'Of course,' Murch pointed out mildly enough, 'he was not aiming to kill you.'

'No, he shoot with his eyes shut!' Kashvili agreed uproariously. 'But brave boy all the same. What do you say, Mr Coombesy?'

'A lucky escape.'

Kashvili laid down his ham sandwich and, after retying a scabbed and bloody bandage, hitched up his trousers. Wiping his fingers on his beard, he swigged from the neck of a very good hock and burped like a sea-lion. 'Now we go to the bank,' he said.

Coombes's mew was like a terrified kitten. 'But surely you understand, I can't let you rob Sir William's deposit boxes in broad daylight. On a Saturday. At hardly past ten in the morning.'

'Coombesy, you don't got no choice. What is thing here, at end of table?'

'A mincing machine.'

'I put your hand in machine, turn handle. Which hand we start with? You choose.'

'But the pearls are not yours,' Coombes yelped.

'No, but for sure they are not his,' Kashvili countered. 'I don't got no wish to harm you, old man. Is just business. Every thing will work out good. You'll see.'

'I should do as he says,' Murch advised. 'On account of you don't have much of a choice. He knows you hold the keys somewhere in the house and there's no sense in getting knocked about for them.'

'You see?' Kashvili boomed. 'This fellow understands good. Better we go together, like old friends. You give me red box with pearls, I kiss you big goodbye, go back on to my ship, pfft.'

'Except that Judd will have seen the ship at anchor and made plans of his own,' Murch objected quietly.

'Possible,' Kashvili shrugged. 'But he don't know it's my ship.'

'He's a nosey bastard. The longshoremen saw you come in, I don't doubt. Word'll get back quick enough. No, this is the plan. You bring Mr

216

Coombes and the pearls back here and we wait for him.'

'You try to tell me what I got to do, English?'

'Your pal killed a woman a week ago. Yesterday he tried to kill another. After you've gone and he's left to himself he will do some damage to Mr Coombes here. Then he'll come after you. That don't sit well with me, any of it. You get him back here and I will finish him.'

'You?' Kashvili laughed.

'Look into my eyes,' Murch said quietly. 'What do you see?'

The Georgian thought about it.

*   *   *

'Well, you have been in the wars!' Millie Rogerson said six days later. She and Murch lay in the attic bedroom of the house in Chiswick a little after dawn, a wonderful light in the sky and air as crisp as champagne. She was the same sardonic Millie but with some newly added catch of caution in her voice. For, seen against white sheets and more especially her own flawless nakedness, Murch did indeed look like a man who had been blown off a ladder at the Malakoff Redoubt (an event that had actually happened to him in the last days of the Crimean campaign).

'Like they told you, I was set upon by footpads,' he explained patiently. 'You expect a tussle or two with that sort of work.'

'My eye,' Millie said derisively. 'Mr Kennett has been wringing his hands the past week, crying woe on his mate Westland for leaving you in the lurch. Not that it hasn't all turned out for the best. That

217

old Sir William is back in London, did you know that?'

'I did not.'

'Had the four of them to dinner Thursday night in Cadogan Square. All smiles there again, though if he knew the mischief his daughter was up to he might change his tune.'

'There's mischief, is there?'

'Well, not of the unheard-of kind. But it would be better the lovebirds married as soon as may be. You follow my drift, Murchie.'

'I think I've got the picture. Mr Kennett hasn't fallen out with his mate serious, has he?'

'Do I listen at doors?' she protested, laughing.

'I hope you do,' Murch said, swinging his leg over the side of the bed and standing up with only a few concealed winces. He walked to the open window and hung on the frame, gasping.

Millie watched him, her lower lip trapped by her teeth. 'You are a rare 'un and no mistake,' she said in a low voice. 'This cove Judd. Where is he now?'

Murch yawned. 'He has gone away,' he replied. It was difficult to be nonchalant with a black eye and a leg that throbbed like a second heart. But if his smile was crooked, it was out of shyness. He had yet to grow used to being naked in front of Millie and for sure he was never at his best in the early morning. She seemed to sense this and jumped out of bed to embrace him, her breasts warm against his narrow chest.

He kissed her. 'Mr Judd was an evil bastard, Millie—neither use nor ornament to the world. But now he's gone away. That's all them downstairs want to hear and the same should be true of you. He has gone.'

'Mrs Wallis knows how,' she warned.

'Thinks she does.'

Not even Bella could imagine the size of hole a duck gun could make in a bad man's heart. In Bella's fiction, there would have been a scene between Murch and the villain, in which the final strings of the plot were tied, followed by finger-wagging denunciations, a few words of civilised regret—and only then the meting out of justice. And although Judd was expecting something of the same kind when he walked through Mr Coombes's kitchen door, Murch had not read too many works of fiction. Coombes's gun was hidden on the table between Mrs Jeavons's cake tins and biscuit barrels, only the muzzle showing. As soon as he crossed the threshold, Murch pulled the trigger and despatched Judd to eternity. The spread of shot had also ruined several copper saucepans.

Kashvili took the corpse on a short cruise north and west to a point off The Carracks, returned on the afternoon tide to Carbis Bay and was rowed ashore in a captain's uniform from the outfitter's next to the Metropole in Rotterdam. He was, he explained to a tearstained Agnes Skillane, her husband's surprise guest and brought with him the compliments of all the other captains of the Skillane fleet. Mary's absence and Judd's disappearance had thrown elements of doubt over that evening's banquet; but Kashvili knew how to enjoy a party. When a greatly shaken Coombes arrived in ancient evening dress, the Georgian embraced him like an old friend, lifting him off his feet and kissing him exuberantly on both cheeks.

*　　　*　　　*

219

'Anyoldhow,' Murch asked now, his face in Millie's hair. 'How have you been keeping?'

She was distracted from answering by squeals and screams from the garden. Racing around the lawn was an ecstatic Mary Skillane, pursued by William Kennett wafting an enormous butterfly net on a bamboo pole. Like the watchers in the attic, they had just risen from bed.

'Mrs Wallis—' Millie began.

'Ah yes, it's only fit that she should have the last word. What does she say?'

'She says I should take you down to Margate and marry you.'

Then, thought Billy Murch, she does know. Or can guess. 'A wise woman,' he said. 'And at the same time, what Percy Quigley calls a consummate weaver of dreams.'

'Is that a yes?' Millie Rogerson asked.

'Call it a yes,' Murch replied.

She seemed well pleased with the answer and disengaged herself to find her clothes. A thought occurred to her in the act of pulling on her second stocking.

'This foreign cove, this Kashvili you mentioned. He got the pearls then, did he?'

Billy smiled and jerked his thumb at the open window, below which William Kennett and Mary were still scampering and squealing.

'He got the pearls,' he confirmed. 'But they got each other. Same as I got you. It all worked out reasonable, I would say.'

Millie studied him with the half-mocking smile he would come to know so well, the one that disguised her truest feelings about him for fear of spoiling the perfect man. Billy shrugged his shoulders humorously and walked across the bedroom carpet towards the perfect woman. Oh yes, the perfect woman. Said as much, dizzy with love.

*   *   *

In Orange Street on the same shiny morning, Bella sat up in bed with a small oblong package tied with lawyers' red tape. Philip watched her scrabbling at the gift paper with which it was wrapped.

'How have I earned this?' she asked. 'It is you who commanded us with such skill in Cornwall and you who deserve the reward.'

'I wish that were so on both counts,' Philip murmured. 'That we came out of it with our lives is something, I suppose. Saving the girl was also a good thing, and of course joining Kennett with Mary Skillane has been a spectacular success.'

'You might sound a little more pleased with yourself, therefore,' she scolded.

'Never to set foot in Cornwall again will be reward enough for me.'

The last of the paper came away from the package and Bella was left with a silver cardboard box. She opened it and peered inside.

'It is a stylograph,' Philip explained. 'Or, more accurately, an American stylograph. I'm told by the man who sold it to me that over there it is absolutely the *dernier cri*. Inkwells are a thing of the past, pen wipers, ancient history. In ordinary terms, it is a reservoir pen. This particular one is the invention of Mackinnon and Cross. Mackinnon should by rights be a sandy-haired Scottish inventor, but is, I'm told, a Canadian bigwig moonlighting in New York.'

'But it's wonderful!' Bella exclaimed. 'Why is there no ink?'

'There is ink but it is hidden in the barrel of the pen.'

'If it's there it's very shy!' She gave a few cheerful flicks and decorated the sheets, the pillow and the exposed part of Philip's chest.

'What a very romantic gift,' she said, kissing him and wondering how best to hide the stylograph in the weeks ahead. Such things could never replace the penholder and the inkpot. She wondered sometimes at how foolish the world was becoming. Without a blackened callus on the second joint of the middle finger, Henry Ellis Margam would cease to be. Perhaps, unconsciously or not, that was what Philip Westland had in mind.

222

CHIVERS
LARGE
PRINT
—direct—

If you have enjoyed this Large Print book and would like to build up your own collection of Large Print books, please contact

Chivers Large Print Direct

Chivers Large Print Direct offers you a full service:

• Prompt mail order service

• Easy-to-read type

• The very best authors

• Special low prices

For further details either call Customer Services on (01225) 336552 or write to us at Chivers Large Print Direct, **FREEPOST**, Bath BA1 3ZZ

Telephone Orders:
FREEPHONE 08081 72 74 75